Sweet
CHRISTMAS
Love

Sweet CHRISTMAS Love

BARBARA GLOVER
SUZANNE LIEURANCE
WENDY DEWAR HUGHES

CREATIVE CARAVAN PRESS

Sweet Christmas Love

Published in Canada by Creative Caravan Press.

Editing by Suzanne Lieurance, Write by the Sea Press; Wendy Dewar Hughes, Summer Bay Press; Julene Schroeder, Editing Excellence.

Book design by Wendy Dewar Hughes, Summer Bay Press.
Cover art by Wendy Dewar Hughes, Summer Bay Studio.
Cover design by Wendy Dewar Hughes, Summer Bay Press.

ISBN: 978-1-927626-38-2
Digital ISBN: 978-1-927626-39-9

A kiss is a lovely trick designed by nature to stop speech when words become superfluous.

Ingrid Bergman

CHRISTMAS IN LULULAND

Wendy Dewar Hughes

The snow had begun to fall by the time Elliott Robinson turned off the evening news. It came down in soft twirling flakes at first but before long lay in a thick carpet on the sidewalks and drifted heavily down through the glow of the streetlights. Before morning the wind picked up and had swirled all that fallen snow and more into drifts, which covered the front walk and formed crescents in the corners of the veranda of Elliott's house.

Elliott looked at the clock on the stove at 7:34 and decided that if he hurried he had exactly eleven minutes in which to sweep the porch steps and shovel the walk.

He did not like to hurry but he zipped his parka, yanked the earflaps of his fur-lined hat down to his chin and pulled on his gloves. Outside, a blast of cold air hit him with stinging needles of snow as he grabbed the broom, which miraculously still stood in the corner behind a snow-filled flowerpot on the veranda. With the straw broom, its bristles worn down almost to the strings, he dispatched the snow piled on the steps, then switched to the snow shovel that he kept tucked behind the little spruce tree and flung the drifts from the walkway. It wouldn't do to go off to work having the house look like he'd let it go.

At exactly 7:45 Elliott locked his front door and set off. Five minutes later, he turned a key in the front door of Robinson's Hardware and let himself in. The bell over the door tinkled as he pushed the door closed against the bitter wind and went to turn off the alarm and switch on the lights. He could see his breath but once he edged up the thermostat, it would warm up. Elliott Robinson would never have described himself as parsimonious. He simply placed great importance on getting value for his money.

Forty-five minutes later, Ethel Martins blew through the store's door, setting the bell jangling again, and marched up to where Elliott stood behind the counter sorting bolts by size.

"Elliott," she snapped, "turn up that heat or I'm going to turn right around and go home. How do you expect a woman to work a computer when her fingers are frozen to the keyboard?"

Elliott stared at her for a full minute. He and Ethel had this disagreement nearly every morning. In winter it was about the heat; in summer it was the air conditioning.

"I've already cranked it up to sixty-five degrees," he said stiffly. He pushed his black-framed glasses up on his nose and studied how the wind had rearranged Ethel's mauve hair into drifts that resembled those on the sidewalks.

"If you won't turn it up, then I will!" she declared, and went straight to the thermostat and gave the lever a push. When she stomped into the back room to hang up her purse and coat, Elliott stepped to the wall and turned it back down, then calmly went back to sorting bolts.

Elliott placed the boxes of bolts in their slots on the shelf and pulled out several bins of washers. Why people couldn't put them back where they'd taken them from he didn't know. It irked him something fierce when things were out of place. He was about to set the bins on the counter when the front door burst open, setting the bell clanging and flying all the way back so it banged into a stack of neatly arranged cans of paint.

"Oh, my goodness," said a muffled voice as a woman in a bright pink coat reached for and pushed the door closed against the blast of winter wind. "A girl could get blown right off her feet out there today," she cried, brushing snow from the front of her coat with one hand. In the other hand she carried a heavy, black case. She wore tall black boots with heels so high that Elliott had to wonder how she could navigate on them even on days when the sun shone and the sidewalk was dry and smooth, much less on a day like today. The woman set her case on the floor, pulled off a pair of cobalt blue gloves and, spreading her fingers, ran her hands up into a mass of windblown, pale blonde curls. Giving her head a shake, she said, "That's better," then swept up the case and marched over to where Elliott stood, her hips swaying and those heels tapping on the linoleum tile floor.

"Good morning," she said, her deep pink lips curving into a wide smile. "Are you the manager?" She blinked her wide blue eyes and Elliott could see melted snow sparkling on her long, black lashes. He sucked in his stomach and straightened, pressing his shoulders back.

"I'm the owner of Robinson's, ma'am. How may I help you?"

She stuck out her hand with fingers that were tipped in long, bright pink nails with something sparkly on them and said, "My name is Lulu Davis. I'm the sales rep with Gifts Aplenty Agency. I represent eighteen different giftware lines. If you have a few minutes I can show you my catalogues and help you get some more merchandise in your store. I know the season is getting a little late but see by your windows that you must have already sold out of your Christmas stock so you'll want to order more right away before the real rush starts."

Elliott took her hand in his and she gave it a firm shake. He wasn't sure but he thought she even winked at him. She leaned over to where she had set her case by her feet and Elliott leaned, too.

She popped back upright, pushing a big looping curl from her eyes and slid the bins of washers out of the way. She dropped an armful of catalogues and binders on the counter. "You haven't told me your name yet, honey," she said, leaning a little toward Elliott, just close enough so he could inhale her perfume. *Something musky and exotic,* he thought, but what would he know?

"I'm, uh, I'm Elliott, Elliott," he said, unsure why his mouth chose this moment to stop working properly. "Uh, Elliott Robinson." He waved a hand vaguely toward the front of the store to indicate the sign over the door. "Uh, I am sorry, miss, but I don't need any more stock for Christmas…" He trailed off, staring at how her eyebrows shot up into perfect crescents over her sparkling blue eyes. *How did a person ever get eyes that blue?* he wondered.

Lulu Davis turned around and surveyed the store, one hand on her hip and the other tapping the counter with those long nails. "Elliott, honey, I know you're putting me on. Look at those windows." She flung a hand in the direction of the display windows, one side decorated with three paint cans and the other with snow shovels and sacks of road salt. "How do you expect to get anyone in here to shop for Christmas when your front windows look like that?" She swung around and tilted her head to one side, gazing into Elliott's grey eyes. He cleared his throat and pushed up his glasses.

"Now, just have a look at this catalogue for five minutes and in only a few days you and I will have those front windows transformed into a holiday wonderland.

Every woman in town is going to be in here buying toys for the children, gifts for daughters, sisters, and moms, and guy stuff for their men."

"But, but, they all usually go to the mall in Painesville," Elliott stuttered. "Nobody shops for Christmas here. "

Lulu laid a slender hand on Elliott's sweatered arm. "It's easy to see why, Elliott, honey, when there's nothing for them to buy." Her voice was soft with sympathy and she gazed into his eyes again and gave a long, slow blink.

An hour and a half later, Elliott Robinson had ordered more than three thousand dollars worth of giftware, Christmas decorations, toys, woollen scarves, men's boxed shirt and tie sets, jewellery boxes, bath products, and three fully flocked Christmas trees, complete with all the trimmings. When Ethel emerged from the back office to give the thermostat another push, Elliott informed her that he was going out for lunch with Miss Lulu Davis and would return in one hour.

Open-mouthed, Ethel watched Elliott don his coat and gloves and usher the big-haired, shapely, long-legged, bright-pink-lipped, eyelash-flapping woman out the door. In the entire forty-two years that she had known him, from the time he wore diapers, she had never seen him look like that. She saw him smooth down his dark brown curls, the only wild thing about him, as he closed the door and headed down the street toward Clayton's Café with Lulu Davis' hand tucked firmly in the crook of his arm.

Ethel's head wagged back and forth as Elliott disappeared from sight. Then she sniffed and muttered, "That woman has 'gold-digger' written all over her."

CHAPTER TWO

After struggling against the bitter wind that swept down Delamere's main street, Clayton's Café felt warm and welcoming to Lulu Davis. The scent of bacon and cinnamon buns and hot coffee drifted past her as Elliott steered her smoothly toward a booth near the back. She slid onto the red leatherette seat and plopped her leopard-print purse down beside her. She looked across the table at Elliott Robinson.

Lulu had met lots of men like Elliott in her going-on-five-years as a giftware sales rep. They owned mom and pop stores in little towns all over her territory. They were good, honest people for the most part but the orders they placed barely afforded her enough commission to live on. Not that she complained; she enjoyed life too much to waste any time griping about her lot, and she loved the gift business and the travel. But lately she had felt herself wanting something else — a real home and a family — before it was too late. At thirty-four, Lulu knew that time was running out if she ever hoped to hold a child of her own in her arms.

"You want menus, El?" a woman called from over the swinging half-doors that separated the kitchen from the rest of the café.

"Sure, Tammy," Elliott answered over his shoulder.

Lulu saw the woman give an exaggerated roll of her eyes before grabbing a couple of plastic-covered menus and slapping them down on the table. "Coffee?" she offered Lulu.

"No, thanks," Lulu answered, smiling big. "It makes me all jittery."

"Well," Tammy said, "we wouldn't want that now, would we? I'll be back in a minute to take your order. You want the same as always, El?"

Elliott nodded as Tammy strode back into the kitchen.

"You must come here all the time," Lulu said to Elliott, tilting her head.

"Everyday, almost."

"So tell me about your store," she prompted. "Have you owned it for long?"

Elliot pressed his wayward curls down against his head again. "My father left it to me. I've owned it since I was twenty-two years old. That was the year he died of a heart attack," Elliott explained as he twirled a fork in one hand. "Oddly enough, my grandfather died at the same age as my father did, forty-two."

"I'm so sorry," Lulu said, reaching across the table to squeeze Elliott's wrist briefly. "That must have been difficult for you."

Elliott shrugged. "It wasn't easy taking over the store that young," he said. "After mom passed away, I took over the house, too."

Lulu could see a flush start up Elliott's neck. She hated to see anyone uncomfortable and usually started talking as a diversion from further anxiety or embarrassment. Elliott Robinson was not a supremely handsome man but his face had a kind of sensitivity, like someone who had known pain. She could see it in his eyes. Lulu believed that you could tell a lot about someone from his eyes if you really looked. Sometimes she would study her customers, store owners or buyers, and just knew whether they would pay on time or if they were the type to make the company wait sixty, ninety, or even a hundred and twenty days to pay a net-thirty invoice. Looking at Elliott now, she knew he was not one of those.

"I never knew my father," she said. "My mom was only sixteen when she had me and he was long gone before then." She said it without remorse. It was an old story but it was her story. "She left not long after so I grew up with my grandmother. My own grandfather died when I was young and I was eight when Gran died. After that I went into foster care and saw my mom about once a year until I was fifteen. That's when I ran away, got a job, finished high school, went to college, got married for about five minutes and got divorced. The first time he blackened my eyes it was over, and well, here I am." She shrugged and spread her hands out, palms up.

Tammy showed up to take her order.

"That makes my life seem like a piece of cake," Elliott remarked. "And your mom named you Lulu?"

She laughed. "Goodness no! She named me Louetta-Louise Lootendorfer. She thought it was cute. Good grief, right? I changed it to Lulu the moment I could talk. The only good thing that skunk of a guy I married gave me was a last name that wasn't Lootendorfer."

Elliott laughed out loud. He hardly ever did that. When their food arrived, his order turned out to be a grilled ham and cheese sandwich on rye bread and a side salad with Italian dressing — the exact same thing that she had ordered.

"How freaky is that!" Lulu cried when Tammy set the plates down. Elliott just smiled.

"How long will you be in Delamere," he asked a while later as he pushed his empty plate away.

"Well, I planned to be here only for the morning but it looks like fate had other plans. I hit a patch of black ice coming into town, spun around about three times and smacked into a light post. The guys at the garage told me it could take up to a week before they get the parts to fix my car so I guess I'm stuck. I'd catch the bus and go back to the city but there's nothing waiting for me there." Elliott saw her shoulders sag. "I guess I'll just get a room at that little inn I saw up the road and consider this a surprise vacation. It's getting too late in the season for sales anyway. This was going to be my last trip until after the New Year when the gift shows start."

"There's not much to do in Delamere," he said, "especially when the weather's bad."

"Oh, you don't have to worry about me," she said, waving his concern away. "As long as there's a library, or even a drugstore with a spinner full of paperbacks I can occupy myself. Besides, I've already submitted all your orders and they should start arriving in a couple days. I can help you unpack and merchandise everything."

Her eyes sparkled as she proceeded to suggest all the ways they could decorate the store together. When it came time to pay the bill, Elliott slid a twenty across the table to Tammy to cover the $12.99 their lunches cost and told her to keep the change. Tammy's eyes bulged and her mouth dropped open but, with one severe look from Elliott, she backed away. He held out his hand to help Lulu to her feet, tucked her arm in against his side and led her out of the restaurant.

Tammy watched them go without moving until they were out of sight. Then she picked up the phone and punched in some numbers.

"Ethel," she said, "you're not going to believe what just happened to me. Elliot left me a seven-dollar tip."

"We're going to have to put a stop to whatever might be fixin' to go on," Ethel snapped, "before it has a chance to get started."

CHAPTER THREE

Tammy Carter tucked that seven-dollar tip into the pocket of her jeans and allowed herself a tiny smile. She had seen the look in Elliott's eyes as he gazed across the table at that blowsy blonde woman. She too wanted to nip in the bud any attraction that might be starting to simmer between those two.

Tammy and Elliott had known each other since they were children and had grown up together through all their school years in Delamere. She wasn't in love with him but as life-long friends, she thought they would make a good match. Since the love of her life had taken off a few years before with that woman from Painesville, Tammy had been scrambling just to get by. Her two children had finished high school and gone off to college but the bills never ended. Tammy knew from bits of information provided by Ethel, Robinson's Hardware's bookkeeper, that while Elliott may not like to *spend* money, that didn't mean he didn't *have* money.

A few weeks earlier, Tammy had slid into the booth opposite where Elliott sat having his lunch.

"Hey, El," she said, "I've been thinking."

"Oh?" Elliott answered through his grilled ham and cheese. She saw his brow furrow. Not a good sign. She decided she might as well jump in with both feet.

"We've known each other a long time, we're both single, and we're not getting any younger, either of us. Maybe you and I should, you know, think about our futures. Maybe we could have a future together..."

Elliott gulped and gagged a bit, as if he had forgotten to chew the bite of sandwich in his mouth. His eyes watered and he took a big swallow of water. "Are you suggesting we get married?" he asked when he had caught his breath.

"Uh, well yeah, maybe," Tammy stammered, "something like that."

Elliott reached across the table and took Tammy's hand in his. "That's a nice thought, Tam," he said, "but I don't think it would work. We're probably better off the way things are."

When he had finished his meal, she watched him leave the restaurant. "It might be better for you," she muttered, "but I doubt that it will be better for me." She pushed herself onto her sore feet and went back into the kitchen.

After a few days the snowstorm abated and the deliveries of Christmas stock for Robinson's Hardware began to roll in. First to arrive was the shipment with three white trees for the window displays, complete with all the decorations, tinsel, lights, and dangly ornaments, each set with its own colour scheme.

Lulu called the garage every day to see if her car was ready and was first told that the part would be in the next day, then that the part was on back-order and would be another week. She considered hopping on the bus and heading home but she loved the quiet little inn with its cozy chairs by the fire, the hearty home-cooked breakfasts, and the downy duvet to cuddle under at night. She hadn't had a real vacation for a long time so she decided to make her stay in Delamere her vacation time. She didn't have to rush home to look after a pet and, honestly, she knew that no one would miss her if she never came home at all. Her landlady might start to wonder after a while but she had even left post-dated cheques for the rent for the next six months.

On the fourth day of her stay, she wrapped a thick scarf around her neck and ventured out. The wind had dropped but the clouds hung low like a bad attitude and threatened more snow any minute. Picking her way past icy patches, Lulu walked down Main Street, gazing into store windows and admiring the sparkling wreaths hanging on the charming streetlamps. When she arrived at Robinson's Hardware, all she saw in the windows were piles of boxes, most of them still taped closed. She pushed the door open and entered, the bell tinkling overhead. A few customers nosed around the premises and she could see Elliott behind the counter ringing up a purchase for a man in painters' whites. Within a few minutes the store was empty except for Lulu and Elliot. She approached with a smile.

"Hello again, Mr. Robinson," she said.

Elliott looked up. He seemed startled to see her.

"I notice that some of your stock has arrived already," Lulu said, not waiting for him to speak. "I can see that you're busy, and since I'm stuck in town waiting for car parts and with nothing to do, why don't I give you a hand unpacking and merchandising everything? I'm pretty good at window displays."

Elliott glanced at the boxes in the window and scattered on the floor in front of them. "I can't ask you to do that," he said.

"You're not asking," Lulu said. "I'm offering. Not the same thing. I was getting bored at the inn and it looks like I'll be here a while longer. Please give me something to do. . . unless you don't want me to."

He cast another glance at the boxes. "All right, I accept," he said, reaching under the counter and producing a knife to slash the packaging. "Have at it."

Over the next four hours, Lulu unpacked, priced, sorted and set up. First she assembled the white, flocked Christmas trees and placed the large one and the smallest one in one window and the medium-sized one in the other window. Next came the twinkling lights, followed by masses of decorations. The largest tree sported an ornate theme in shades of burgundy and gold; the small tree was dressed in emerald greens and midnight blues. For the tree in the other window, Lulu had suggested a playful theme with multi-coloured characters and baubles, which Elliott had agreed to order, and she now arranged.

Halfway through setting up the windows, the UPS truck arrived and disgorged another dozen boxes of stock. By the time daylight outside began to fade, Lulu was exhausted, but only partway through unpacking and pricing the new stock. With the trees lit, the few townspeople who had ventured out now stopped to admire the Christmas mirage that was taking shape in Robinson's windows.

Elliott too, had been watching the windows transform from a neglected wasteland into a imaginative wonderland and marvelled at Lulu's abilities to turn cardboard boxes full of stuff into such beautiful exhibits. Lulu sat down on the window shelf as Elliott approached.

"They look wonderful," he said, softly. "I could never have done what you have done here."

Ethel strode past yanking her winter coat over her shoulders and tugging on her gloves. "I could have," she said with a snort, "but I notice that you didn't ask me."

"You were too busy," Elliott said, giving her a quizzical look. She had never showed any interest in merchandising stock before in all the years she had worked in the store.

"Well," Ethel jerked open the front door, "you'll never know for sure now, will you? Not with Miss Fancy Lady here doing it for you." With that she slammed the door behind her and marched off down the street.

Elliott cast a sideways glance at Lulu who bit the inside of her bottom lip as she stared after Ethel. She looked back at Elliott and when their eyes met, they burst into laughter.

"I don't know what came over her," Elliott said. "She has never shown the slightest interest in decorating the store."

"'Miss Fancy Lady'?" Lulu said. "I don't think anyone has ever called me that before. I'm not sure whether to be insulted or flattered."

"Let's settle on 'flattered' and go for dinner. It's time to close up anyway."

They chose the Chinese restaurant on the corner and ordered ginger beef, lemon chicken, and fried rice, sitting across from one another in a tiny booth near the front window. Only one other couple shared the restaurant on the chilly evening. By now almost no one was out on the slippery streets and it had begun to snow again. Over tiny cups of green tea, Lulu and Elliott discovered that they both liked many of the same books, had similar tastes in politics, and each attended church on Sundays, singing in the choir.

"I love opera," Elliott said, "though I hardly ever get to go to a real one. It's hard to get away from the store, even for an evening."

"I love opera too," Lulu cried. "I have season's tickets. It's my big self-indulgent splurge. I buy two passes so that I can invite a friend but often I end up going alone anyway." Then her face lit up. "Why don't you come with me when the next one is on?"

"I have a good idea," Elliott said. "The college over in Painesville is performing the Rimsky-Korsakov opera called *Christmas Eve*. Have you ever seen it? If we go to the Sunday performance, the store will be closed."

"It's a date," Lulu agreed.

When Elliott offered to walk Lulu back to the inn, she considered refusing but the wind had picked up again outside and heavy snow slashed down the street at a sharp angle. Besides, she liked Elliott a lot and when he offered her his arm as they headed down the windswept sidewalk, she took it, snuggling close to him against the biting gusts.

At the inn's carved wooden door, they stopped beneath the glow of an old-fashioned coach lamp. "I had a great time this evening," Elliott said, taking Lulu's hands in his. "And you don't know how much I appreciate what you're doing with the store. I just hope the weather clears so that people will venture out to shop."

"Look at it this way," she replied. "If it doesn't clear, no one will be going off to the mall in Painesville. They'll want to shop locally and you'll be the only store in town."

He grinned. "It could work," he said. "Something is going to have to happen for me to sell all the stock before Christmas."

"Don't you worry, honey," Lulu replied. "Once I've finished dressing up the place, no one will be able to resist coming into your store. It will be like a Christmas wonderland." Then she put her two gloved hands on the sides of his face and kissed him. Before he realized what had happened, she'd opened the inn door and disappeared inside.

He stood on the veranda under the coach lamp and pressed his lips together, savouring the sensation of hers on his.

On the street, a car crept past and Tammy stared sideways out the drivers' side window. She could have sworn that she had just seen Elliott kissing that Lulu woman on the steps of The Coach Light Inn.

CHAPTER FOUR

Within a couple of days all the stock that Elliott had ordered under Lulu's coaching had arrived and she had spent happy hours unpacking and sorting the decorations, toys, glassware, jewellery and even a line of purses that Elliott had been skeptical about but Lulu had insisted would sell. "In fact, I'll buy the first one," she told him when she unwrapped them. "I've had my eye on this style all season but I can't get just one."

"Take it," he replied, to Ethel's astonishment. "Take anything you like. You're a marvel and worth every cent I'm paying you."

Lulu stopped sorting a line of key chains featuring dogs and cats and looked up at him. "You're not paying me," she said.

"Of course I will pay you," Elliott objected.

"No, you won't. I'm doing this because I love doing it, and because I'm stuck here until my car gets fixed. You're doing me a favour."

From her vantage point behind the counter, Ethel listened to and eyed the two of them. Then she slipped into the office and picked up the phone. Through the tinted glass separating the office from the retail floor she kept an eye on Elliott but he seemed in no hurry to leave Lulu alone.

"Tammy," she said into the phone, her voice barely above a whisper, "I think it's time to launch our strategy. I've been doing a little investigating and you're going to love what I've dug up."

Two days later, when Lulu had received and priced every one of Elliott's orders and had put the finishing touches on the displays, Ethel decided the time was right. With the heavy cloud cover, darkness came even earlier than it usually did for this time of year. At fifteen minutes before five, Ethel emerged from the back office and stopped next to Elliott at the counter where he tinkered with a faucet handle.

"I sure hope all that Christmas stock sells," she began. "There's an awful lot of it. What are you going to do if no one comes in to buy it?"

"It'll sell," Elliott said without looking up.

"I heard via the grapevine that our Miss Lulu has talked a lot of other stores into buying huge orders and they've been left with most of it to mark down after Christmas."

"Who told you that?" Elliott asked, frowning.

"Oh, I have my connections in the retail world," she replied. "I've been at this a long time." Elliott wondered briefly if she meant at the business of retail or the business of snooping into other people's lives. While she was as reliable a bookkeeper as anyone could want, she had a fondness for meddling that set his teeth on edge.

"What else have you heard from your so-called connections?" he asked sharply.

Ethel looked coy and smiled at him as innocently as a Sunday School teacher. "Now that you ask, I heard that she was married before."

"So?"

This response wasn't what Ethel had been expecting but she took it in stride. "Something, shall we say, shady, went on, apparently."

"I know," Elliott replied, turning to face her. "Her husband was a thief and a petty criminal and he beat her, but only once. She left him after that one and only time. She told me all about it. Her mother ran off, leaving her with her grandparents to raise, then her grandfather died when she was just a little girl."

"Oh," Ethel said, pursing her lips as if they had a drawstring. Elliott read disappointment in her face.

"Well," she said, drawing herself up, "I just thought you should know."

"Why?"

"She just might not be everything she seems, that's all. And I thought I ought to warn you."

"You can go home now," Elliott told her shortly, turning back to the faucet in his hand. "I'll lock up."

After Ethel had gone, stony-faced and silent, her nose wrinkled like she had encountered a bad smell, Elliott locked the door and did his rounds turning off the lights. He left the tree lights on and they glowed out into the street, sparkling off the swirling snow. The windows looked beautiful and customers had already begun trickling in, complimenting him on how nice it was to have such a gorgeous gift selection right here in Delamere this year. Sales on the new product lines were picking up as were sales of the regular hardware stock. People who didn't usually shop in Robinson's came in because of the gift and Christmas lines and left with articles they normally bought elsewhere. As he flipped the cover from the alarm he wondered again what Ethel was thinking. He didn't like this nasty side of her and he wouldn't put up with it in his store or in his private relationships.

With his index finger poised to press in the alarm code, he realized that for the first time in his adult life, he might actually be in the start of a personal relationship, of the romantic kind. He had spent several evenings since Lulu came to town either sharing dinner with her or having short text conversations about books or opera or the bad weather. He had spoken with her every day and when she had been working in his store, he neglected other work so he could talk to her while she worked. He loved watching how her hands with their pink-polished nails gently arranged each article or ornament so it looked just right. She often set up an entire line of products then re-arranged all the pieces so that they were all displayed to the best advantage.

The day before, Elliott and Lulu had attended the matinee performance of *Christmas Eve* at the college as planned. There had been enough of a break in the weather for the roads to open and Elliott had driven the two of them in his immaculate, if not exactly new, pickup truck. Afterward, they went for dinner at a tiny Italian restaurant and when they returned to Delamere, they had spent nearly an hour getting chillier and chillier sitting in the truck and talking about everything from the soprano's high notes to what trees grew best in the local climate.

The conversation was so scintillating that neither realized the passage of time. Lulu had snuggled close to Elliott to stay warm and his arm came around her shoulders. With his face just inches from her tumble of hair, he found the scent of her perfume intoxicating like nothing he had ever experienced before. He closed his eyes and inhaled deeply, wanting the scent of her to fill him up.

After a minute or two he realized that she had asked him a question and when he opened his eyes he saw her face tilted up to his. Without thinking, he lowered his lips to hers and kissed her, first softly then more deeply. Finally, despite the heat they created with their growing passion, the winter temperatures had won out and they said goodnight.

Now Elliott stood poised to punch in the store's alarm code numbers, savouring the memory and tasting Lulu's sweetness again. His cell phone tinkled in his pocket. He pulled it out and saw Lulu's name on the display.

"Hey, Lu," he said.

"Hey, you too. Want to come over to the inn and watch a movie with me? They're showing Christmas oldies and it's surprise night. The invitation includes gooey cinnamon buns and hot chocolate. Will you come?"

Elliott couldn't think of any other place he'd rather be on a night like this, than in the circle of warmth that surrounded Lulu. Just the thought of sitting next to her on the big overstuffed sofa in the inn's lounge filled him with a warm glow. As he set the alarm and turned the key in the lock to secure the store, he suddenly realized something that shocked him to the core. He was falling in love with Lulu Davis.

On the other side of town, Tammy sat across the kitchen table from Ethel in Tammy's little house behind the Big Bubble Laundromat.

"I tried, Tammy," Ethel explained. "He already knew and he wasn't fazed a bit. It's like he didn't care if she was something the cat dragged in after a night of carousing. We're going to have to move on to Step Two since Step One didn't have the desired effect."

"Okay," said Tammy. "I'm going to have to go through my closet and see what I can find. And with this weather, it's not easy to look desirable when you're wearing a parka and mukluks. "

"Invite him over for supper, silly," Ethel coached. "Elliott's too polite to turn you down. "

"I guess I could. . . " Tammy said. "And I have that little red dress I got for the restaurant Christmas party last year. "

"Do you want to live here the rest of your life?" Ethel asked, raising a pointed eyebrow as she glanced around Tammy's tiny kitchen.

Tammy sighed. "Not on your life. "

CHAPTER FIVE

Just when it looked like the weather would break and the sun might come out again, another Arctic front slashed down from the north bringing more snow, colder temperatures and fierce winds. Weather advisories warned everyone not to travel, followed by road closures due to blizzard conditions. The highway to Painesville closed to all traffic save the snowploughs and even they ceased to run when visibility dropped to zero. Then the power went out. High winds coupled with heavy snow downed trees and felled lines.

Robinson's Hardware kept the lights on and the heat high because, while the rest of the town shivered in the dark, Robinson's had its own generator. Elliott wanted it toasty warm so Lulu wouldn't catch a chill. Not only that but earlier in the fall Elliott had put in a supply of generators that turned his store rooms and basement into a series of tunnels through boxes containing power generators of every size.

People swarmed the store, leaving their cars and pickup trucks idling at the curb to keep them from freezing up, and loaded up with generators, plumbing supplies, electrical wiring and, since they couldn't go anywhere else to shop for Christmas, gifts for the entire family. The jewellery and purses that Ethel had sneered at, and had caused Elliott to question his sanity, sold out in a few days. The decorated Christmas trees went from being thick with garlands and ornaments to having to be re-arranged repeatedly to fill in the empty spaces.

Lulu fought the wind and snow every day and walked the three blocks from the inn to Robinson's. She told Elliott that she needed something to do besides sit by the fire and read and told herself that she was just going to help out her new friend in his time of need. Then she told herself that she went to the store daily so that she could be around other people. Eventually, she admitted to herself that it was Elliott she wanted to be with and didn't mind if no one else came within shouting distance. In fact, while she was thrilled at Elliott's success with the products she had sold him, she would have been happier if the two of them could have just been alone together.

With the power down, Tammy's scheme to invite Elliott for an intimate candlelight dinner at her house went right down the drain. Or it would have, had her pipes not been frozen. She had no generator and no money to buy one. Ethel, however, did have one. She had used her staff discount to put one in a few years earlier so her house still had heat and running water. For the duration, until the power lines were repaired, Tammy moved into Ethel's spare bedroom.

"This isn't looking good," Tammy complained one night after sharing a store-bought frozen pizza with Ethel while they watched re-runs of Magnum PI on television. "Elliott hardly ever comes into the cafe nowadays because he's so busy at the store. I don't know what he's eating for lunch. " She wiped her fingers on a piece of paper towel.

"Floozy-Lu has been bringing him sandwiches and treats from The Coach Light Inn every day," replied Ethel, rolling her eyes. "We're going to have to enact Step Three now, otherwise we might be too late. Elliott looks like a sick calf half the time. Lulu has wrapped him right around her painted-up little pinkie finger. If she comes on the scene for good, my retirement bonus might fly right out the window. After forty-three years at that store, I'm not letting anything get in my way. Fortunately for us, the opportunity dropped in my lap this afternoon."

The following day when Lulu arrived at Robinson's to re-organize the displays again, Ethel caught her attention and called her over with a flick of her finger.

Elliott had gone to the basement to haul up more generators.

"I hate to be the one to mention this to you, sweetie," Ethel began, speaking barely above a whisper, "but I thought you ought to know."

Lulu frowned. "Know what?"

"The clinic called this morning with results of Elliott's tests. " Ethel glanced left and right to make sure no one stood close enough to hear her. "It doesn't sound good."

"What kind of tests?" Lulu wanted to know, trying to remember if Elliott had mentioned having health problems of any kind. She came up blank.

"Well, you know that Elliott's father, God rest his soul, passed away when Elliott was just a young man. He had a congenital heart defect. He died in his early forties and so did *his* father. Seems it runs in the family." She sighed and placed a quivering hand on her chest.

Lulu gasped. "Is this serious?"

Ethel shrugged. "I guess time will tell but I suppose he could go any time." She reached out and patted Lulu on the arm. "I'm sure it's nothing you'll need to worry about though," she said and wandered back into her office.

At lunchtime, Lulu had told Elliott she had to go check on the progress of her car repairs since the long-awaited part had finally made it through the weather. After receiving the news that her car would be ready to drive the next day, she stopped in at Clayton's Café.

"Hi Lulu," Tammy said, sliding a menu onto the table. "Can I pour you some coffee?"

Lulu glanced up at her and nodded. The waitress wore a look of gloom as she sloshed coffee into the mug. "What's wrong?" Lulu asked, genuinely concerned.

"Oh, nothing really…well, I suppose I can tell you." She slid into the booth opposite Lulu. "I had some bad news today. Apparently, Elliott's health isn't very good. I think it's something to do with his heart. His dad died young, you know."

"Yes, I heard," Lulu replied, now becoming troubled. *Could Elliott really be dying,* she wondered.

"Well," Tammy said with a sigh, "I guess there's not much they can do about it. Seems it runs in the family. What can I get for you?"

Lulu glanced at the unopened menu lying on the table. "Just the coffee," she said. Suddenly, she didn't feel very hungry.

CHAPTER SIX

As promised, Lulu's car was ready to pick up at 8:30 the next morning. She paid the bill with her credit card and slid behind the steering wheel, thankful that the car had been indoors all night. After stopping back at The Coach Light Inn and checking out, she pulled the car out onto Main Street. As much as it pained her, she knew what she had to do.

The bell tinkled over the door as she stepped inside Robinson's Hardware for the last time. She had really grown to love this place. By now most of the Christmas gift stock had been sold and the decorations had grown sparse on the once-loaded trees in the windows. Lulu gazed fondly at the displays she had created that now appeared well picked-over. She loved setting up the exhibits and realized that she had a real flare for it. *Well,* she thought, *that doesn't matter much now.* She knew she couldn't stay, couldn't get in any deeper with a man who might die before, well, before they even had a chance to get to know each other better. Before she could make her special Christmas pudding for him, before they could travel together or even have a family. She sighed. Who was she to think any of that would have ever happened anyway?

She found Elliott at the rear of the store grinding a key. "My car repairs are done," she said when he looked up. "I'm about to hit the road. I just wanted to stop and say good-bye." She knew that she was talking too fast but if she didn't get the words out quickly, she might start to cry. "I had fun working on the windows." She stuck out her hand for him to shake.

Elliott just looked at her outstretched hand as though she had just said something to him in a foreign language. He frowned, perplexed. "You're going home?"

Lulu nodded then dropped her hand.

"Aren't you staying for Christmas?" he asked. "I thought we could go skating together in the park once the wind drops. You haven't even seen my house. I took home decorations from the store and did it up really nice. I've never done that before…" He glanced at the key in his hand. "I was making a key to the store for you."

"I'm sorry, Elliott. I know we've had some fun times together." She glanced away, up an aisle toward the front door where her decorations had hung. A lump formed in her throat and threatened to choke her if she didn't leave soon. "But I have to go, get home, you know." She leaned toward him and kissed his cheek and felt something deep in her chest crack and break into pieces. Then she turned, ran down that aisle and out the front door. Elliott watched her go, simply stunned.

Two days later, after fiddling with a light socket for about an hour longer than it required, Elliott put the socket back in its bin and went to get his coat and hat. He didn't feel like working at all and Ethel could look after the front while he went home for a while to lie down. Before he reached the coat hook, Max Parmin, a local contractor, strode up to the counter and thumped a couple of boxes of nails down.

"How ya doin', Elliott?" Max asked, examining Elliott's face.

Elliott looked up at Max who stood a good half a head taller and said, "Okay. Why?"

"You know, that thing with your ticker. " Max struck his own barrel chest with his fist. "I heard it's not so sound. "

"What are you talking about?"

"I was over at Clayton's yesterday and I overheard Tammy talking to Ethel," he indicated the back office with a tilt of his chin. "I wasn't snooping, mind you. I just couldn't help but hear Ethel tell Tammy that the condition of your heart was pretty bad. Is it the same thing that your dad had?"

"What?" Elliott still couldn't fathom what Max could possibly be talking about. He knew there wasn't a thing wrong with his heart and told Max so.

"Well, I'm glad to hear it," Max said, paying for the nails. As Elliott watched him leave the store, something began to dawn on him. He stepped behind the partition and into the back office where Ethel sat staring at her computer screen.

Leaning against the doorframe, he said, "Did you tell Tammy I have a heart condition?"

"I don't know what you mean," she replied absently.

"I think you do. Look at me." Ethel dragged her gaze away from the screen and reluctantly looked at Elliott. "Did you tell Tammy that I have a bad heart?"

"I might have said something about that possibility. You did have tests recently, didn't you?"

Elliott didn't answer her question. "Did you tell Lulu that I have a bad heart?" He could feel the heat rising up his neck and suddenly knew exactly what had happened. Without waiting for his employee to answer, he grabbed his coat, hat, and keys. "Look after the store while I'm gone," he growled. "I don't know when I'll be back."

It was evening by the time he reached the outskirts of the city and while there had been a bit of drifting snow, once the sun went down and the wind with it, the roads were bare and dry. Now the stars sparkled in the cold night sky like flecks of crystal on black velvet. Elliott found the street overhung with leafless trees festooned with twinkling lights where Lulu had a suite at the back of a grand old house. He parked at the curb and jumped out of his truck, slamming the door behind him.

Jogging around to the back, he yanked off his glove and jabbed the doorbell button. The lights were on in the suite but he heard nothing in response, so he pressed the button again. This time he heard a muffled voice say, "All right, I'm coming." His heart leapt.

Light spilled onto the snow outside as Lulu pulled open the door. She had one hand clutching a fuzzy bathrobe up to her chin.

"Hello, Lulu," Elliott said.

"Elliott," Lulu said softly. "What are you doing here?"

He looked around, first up at the Christmas lights strung across the top of the door then at the tiny evergreen in a pot next to the wall, also decorated like something from a magazine. "I came for you," he said finally, looking straight into her eyes.

"You'd better come in," Lulu said, reaching for his sleeve and drawing him into the warm room. "It's freezing out there."

Once she had closed the door firmly behind him, she stepped away from him and wrapped her arms around her middle. "Please tell me again why you're here."

"I came for you," he said, reaching out and lifting a wild curl away from her cheek. "Since you left, I've been useless. I can't think about anything but you. I can't eat, I put stuff away in the wrong places, I've even priced things wrong. And I'm babbling..." He shoved his hands in his pockets.

"I don't know what to say, Elliott," Lulu confessed. "I've been the very same but," tears sprang to her eyes and she flicked them away with her fingertips, "I don't think I can be with you. I don't think I could bear to lose you."

"Oh, for crying out loud," Elliott said so loudly that Lulu jumped. "Did Ethel tell you that I'm going to die young? Did she tell you that I have some heart condition that's going to kill me any day now?"

Shocked at his outburst, Lulu nodded. "I'm not sure I could stand to lose you, since I've only just found you.

You're the first man I've ever really loved, I mean, *really* loved. The thought of losing you is just too much. "

Elliott reached out and folded her into his arms. "Lulu, my love, there is absolutely nothing wrong with my heart, except that you've stolen it. "

"But," Lulu looked up into his eyes, "Ethel and Tammy both said…"

"I'll deal with them later. " With that his lips met hers and Lulu leaned into his embrace. After several long, love-sweet kisses, Elliott stepped away. "Do you mind if I take my coat off? It's getting hot in here and I have something I need to ask you. "

Lulu hung up his coat and then he guided her to the sofa. She lowered herself to the leather cushions. Dropping to his knee before her he said, "I know we haven't known each other long but I love you. I want you to marry me, to attend all the opera season performances with me, skate in the park with me in winter, and have a family with me. Will you, Lulu? Will you marry me?"

The tenderness in his eyes was almost her undoing, and with tears trickling down her cheeks, she nodded. "Yes, Elliott, I will marry you. I want all those things that you want. And I want them now."

Elliott could barely contain his joy. "How soon can we get married?"

"Well," Lulu answered, "the day after tomorrow is Christmas Eve. How about then?"

"It's a date," Elliott replied, and he kissed her again.

On Christmas Eve, the sun blazed across the sparkling drifts of pristine snow around the little church in Delamere. Elliott and Lulu had spent the previous day shopping for rings; then he had gone back home to arrange with the pastor for the ceremony and with the café for a little reception in their private room in the back. Lulu had shopped for a wedding dress, veil, shoes, flowers, and some new outfits for her wedding night and honeymoon.

It seemed like half of Delamere had shown up for the ceremony since everyone in town had known Elliott all his life. Only a few of Lulu's friends from the city had been able to come out but she didn't care. It was Christmas Eve and she was marrying the love of her life.

As the organist began to play, two figures in the back pew whispered to each other behind cupped hands.

"There goes my pension," Ethel moaned softly, gazing at Elliott standing up at the front of the church in his new tuxedo.

"Yeah, and it looks like I'm going to have to live with that miserable plumbing for the rest of my days," Tammy griped.

Ethel looked at her. "Why don't you just move into my house? It's too big for me alone anyway, and it will cost you a whole lot less. And my heat never goes off."

Tammy turned toward her and thought for a moment. "Okay, I will."

Just then the pastor asked the entire congregation to rise as Lulu appeared at the doorway wearing champagne satin scattered with sparkling crystals and began her slow walk up the aisle towards Elliott.

Tammy leaned over to whisper in Ethel's ear. "It looks like we're going to have Christmas in Lululand from now on."

A BOYFRIEND FOR CHRISTMAS

Suzanne Lieurance

In the early morning the day before Christmas, Amy McKenzie stood in line at the airport in Venice, Italy, waiting to board the plane that would take her back home to the States for the holidays. It would be a long trip with a connecting flight at JFK Airport in New York City, so she had dressed comfortably in a soft oversized emerald green sweater and black yoga pants. Her shoulder-length, dark curly hair was pulled back into a twist with a clip, and oversized black-framed glasses hid her long dark lashes and big green-gray eyes. She had checked one large suitcase—mostly full of presents for her family—and as the line moved, she scooted her carry-on bag forward on the floor with her foot. Her gray coat was draped across her right arm and a huge, soft leather purse hung from her shoulder.

Amy loved living and working abroad as an English teacher in an exclusive private school in a small village outside Venice, where she'd been employed for the past four years but it was such fun going back to her childhood home in Kansas City each December to spend Christmas with her family. Still, every year she longed for someone special to bring home with her. Her younger sister, Julie, never came home from college alone. She had Adam. And even though Amy found Adam somewhat boring and ordinary, she envied Julie and even felt a bit embarrassed that her younger sister had found love while she was still looking. Julie never got those sad looks from their mother that said, "I'm sure you'll have a boyfriend for Christmas one of these days, dear. Just be patient."

A boyfriend for Christmas...now, wouldn't that be nice, Amy mused as the line inched forward. She looked to see how much closer they were getting to the gate and spotted a sandy-haired young man in uniform a few spaces ahead of her.

An American serviceman...a stranger in uniform.

A backpack was slung over his right shoulder and he clutched his boarding pass and passport as if he were afraid they might slip out of his hands. Amy checked to see if he had a traveling companion but, no, he was alone. As she studied his left hand and noticed he was not wearing a wedding ring, butterflies fluttered in her stomach and her heart leapt. She immediately imagined the two of them sitting together on the plane. He'd offer her the window seat, of course. Then he'd ease in next to her, taking the middle seat. They would chat during the entire flight across the Atlantic, so that by the time they arrived in the States they'd know quite a lot about each other and they wouldn't ever want to be apart. This handsome soldier would fall head over heels for Amy once he got to know her. She was sure of it!

Amy suddenly wondered where the soldier was going once they got to New York. That could be his final destination, of course, but he could have a connecting flight to almost anywhere in the country. Amy didn't want to consider that he might not be going to Kansas City, though, so she put that possibility out of her mind. Besides, she was a big believer in fate. That is, if the paper fortune in that odd little Christmas cookie she'd eaten at her school holiday party a few days ago was fate.

The fortune that declared, "A stranger in uniform will lead you to romance."

He has to be the stranger in uniform predicted in my fortune cookie. So he must be going to Kansas City. He just has to be! I'm sure he already has plans for Christmas Day, of course. But we can still get together during the holidays. And I can invite him over to meet Mom and Dad...and Julie. She smiled at the thought of Julie seeing her with such a handsome young man — in uniform, no less.

Won't she be surprised! Surprised? Ha! She'll be shocked!

Next to this serviceman, Adam, who usually wore a baggy sweatshirt and jeans, was a troll. "An absolute troll," Amy mumbled. The woman in line behind her backed away with a puzzled look on her face. Amy smiled reassuringly at her, then immediately started making plans for New Year's Eve.

I'll have to buy a new dress, of course, because I'm sure we'll go to a New Year's Eve party since everyone knows that anyone with a date goes to a party on the most exciting evening of the year! Oh, I hope he'll wear a dress uniform to the party! I'll be the envy of every girl there!

Amy could already hear the band playing *Auld Lang Syne.* She could see the streamers and other colorful decorations, and even feel the champagne bubbles tickle her nose, as they toasted the New Year right before the clock struck twelve and the soldier kissed her. And it would be the most incredible kiss, of course! Amy was sure of it!

Before she knew it, Amy was at the gate and someone was checking her passport and boarding pass and wishing her a pleasant flight. She made her way down the gangway onto the plane humming *Have Yourself a Merry Little Christmas*, and then suddenly stopped.

Oh, no!

The handsome soldier was already settled in a seat…a window seat!

You were supposed to save that seat for me, Amy felt like screaming. But she didn't, of course.

An older couple was seated next to the soldier, leaving no room at all for Amy. This was definitely *not* the romantic picture of a cozy flight across the Atlantic that Amy had created in her mind. But what could she do? She frowned and searched for an empty seat. The closest one was on the aisle, five rows back. She made her way to it, still hoping to catch the soldier's eye before she disappeared into the middle of the plane. Once she got to her seat, she put her coat in the overhead compartment before tucking her carry-on bag and purse under the seat ahead of her. She admired the soldier one last time before she plopped down and buckled her seatbelt, folded her arms across her chest and closed her eyes, wishing this particular airline assigned seats to all its passengers. Surely she'd have been assigned the seat next to the soldier if that were the case. Her fortune had almost come true but then an elderly couple got in the way. Amy realized she must correct this huge mistake before it was too late. She just needed to figure out how. Her mind was spinning when the person seated next to her bumped her elbow.

"Headed home for the holidays?"

Amy's thoughts of the soldier vanished.

Is that person talking to me?

She opened her eyes for the first time since sitting down and pushed her glasses up on her nose. A young man seated next to her was looking at her. She hadn't noticed him before because she'd been fixated on the soldier. But now she studied this man's face — strong, square jaw, hazel eyes behind small wire-framed glasses, curly dark hair falling across his forehead.

Not bad, she thought.

Then she looked at his clothes — a baggy New York Jets sweatshirt and… jeans.

"Adam," she mumbled in disappointment.

The young man leaned towards her. "Excuse me?"

Amy cleared her throat. "I'm sorry. Yes, I'm going home for the holidays...to Kansas City. How about you?"

"Just to New York to visit my parents." He offered a hand to Amy. "I'm Brian Percival."

Amy took his hand, mildly impressed with his firm — but not too firm — handshake.

"Amy McKenzie. Nice to meet you."

They were silent after that. Amy made it clear she didn't feel much like talking. She had a problem to solve, after all. And Brian didn't seem to have anything else to say anyway. Amy went back to concentrating on the soldier. She had to devise a plan for meeting him before he got away. Brian plugged into his MP3 player. After a few minutes, a flight attendant made the rounds, reminding everyone to buckle seatbelts, and stow all bags under the seats or in the overhead bins. They'd be taking off shortly, and then refreshments would be served.

Ah...refreshments. I'd like a cocktail, thought Amy.

Yes, a nice stiff drink would make her feel better. At least she thought it might. She didn't really drink alcohol, so she wasn't sure. But it sounded good. She rummaged around for her purse and took a ten-dollar bill from her wallet. She clutched the money as the plane lifted off the ground.

Soon they were high above the clouds. Amy could tell Brian was listening to Christmas songs on his MP3 player because he kept singing, "Here comes Santa Claus," under his breath every few seconds. Amy wasn't much in the mood for Christmas at the moment. She just wanted the flight attendant to come round with the drink cart.

But wait!

The soldier was getting out of his seat and making his way down the aisle to the little lavatory at the back of the plane.

Here's my chance, thought Amy.

As the soldier passed her seat, she tucked the $10 bill into the waist of her pants, unbuckled her seatbelt and followed him, hoping and praying there'd be a line-up for the lavatory and the soldier wouldn't be able to simply pop right in.

She was in luck! One person—an older man—stood outside the lavatory ahead of the soldier. Amy lined up behind them and made a point of softly bumping into the soldier. He turned to her and smiled. Amy knew she needed to play it cool but her heart was beating wildly and her mouth felt like it was full of cotton.

"Sorry," she muttered.

"No problem, ma'am," said the soldier. He turned back in line.

Amy sighed. He wasn't making this easy. He could have at least *tried* to strike up a conversation.

And what's up with ma'am? Makes me feel 100 years old! Oh, well. Desperate times like this called for desperate measures. She released the clasp from her hair and shook her head. Her dark silky hair fell in soft curls to her shoulders. She removed her glasses and cleared her throat.

The soldier turned to face her again. He gulped at the sight of her fluttering her thick dark eyelashes. "What happened to that other girl? The one who was just here?"

Oh, he's good, thought Amy. *What a tease. He's used to flirting with pretty girls. Well, two can play this game.*

"What other girl?" she asked innocently.

"The one with the glasses," said the soldier.

"That was me," said Amy. She pulled her glasses from behind her back and held them up for him to see.

The soldier's eyes widened. "Really?" he said. "You look so…so different."

Amy smiled seductively. "I do?"

The soldier nodded. "It's a good look, too, ma'am," he said, "your hair down and no glasses, I mean." His eyes sparkled. "I'm Travis, by the way, ma'am, Travis Williams. And you are?"

Amy fluttered her eyelashes a bit more and smiled sheepishly. "Amy McKenzie. Nice to meet you, Travis. But please, don't call me ma'am. It makes me feel ancient. So...where are you headed? Once we get to New York, I mean."

Travis put his hands in his pockets and straightened up a bit. "Oh, just to my family's farm for the holidays. It's a couple of hours outside the city."

Amy's face fell.

What? You're not going to Kansas City? How is that even possible? What about my fortune cookie? There has to be some mistake. Don't you realize we're meant to be together?

She couldn't tell Travis about her odd Christmas cookie and the fortune it contained. He might think she was a little crazy. So all she said was, "How nice."

The door to the lavatory opened and a woman came out. The man ahead of Travis went in.

"And where are you going?" Travis asked Amy. "You sound American, so are you headed back home for the holidays, too?"

Amy nodded. "To Kansas City. My parents and sister are there. "

"Never been to Kansas City," said Travis.

Amy forced a weak smile. "It's a nice place. Not as big as New York, of course. But it has its charms. You should see it sometime."

Like right now, she wanted to shout at him. *Like tomorrow for Christmas!*

"Maybe I will," said Travis.

Maybe you will, indeed, thought Amy, and already the wheels in her head were turning, wondering if a relationship with Travis Williams was even possible now that she'd only be seeing him for a few hours on this plane before he drove off to some farm in New York and she boarded another flight for Kansas City.

The door to the lavatory clicked open again and the man who'd been in there held the door for Travis.

"Ladies first," said Travis, and he motioned to Amy.

"Oh, no, that's okay," she said. "I was just going to wash my hands anyway. But now that I think about it, I'm sure I have some wet wipes in my purse. You go ahead. I see the flight attendant coming round with the refreshment cart. I think I'll go get something. Maybe I'll see you later, Travis."

As she walked off, she put her glasses back on and twisted her hair back up and secured it with the clip. A few seconds later, she plopped down next to Brian. He removed his ear buds when he noticed the look on her face. "You okay? You look like you just lost your best friend?"

Much worse, thought Amy. *I've probably just lost the love of my life.*

"I want a drink," she said as the flight attendant appeared with the refreshment cart.

"What would you like?" asked the attendant.

Amy had no idea. She never drank mixed drinks and she didn't like beer.

"Some wine," she said, after much thought. "Some red wine."

Amy pulled the $10 bill from her waistband and paid for her drink. Brian ordered a German beer that he let Amy know was his favorite.

Whatever, she thought. *Doesn't matter to me what you drink.*

An older man who sat on the other side of Brian slept peacefully as Brian and Amy companionably nursed their drinks. Amy slowly relaxed. By the time she had finished her wine, she felt light-headed and sleepy. She'd been up most of the night before packing, and now her lack of sleep was catching up with her. She yawned, and as she closed her eyes, her head fell onto Brian's shoulder.

Several hours later Amy opened her eyes, wondering where she was, snuggled up against someone — someone wearing a New York Jets sweatshirt, someone snoring slightly.

Oh, my gosh! She sat up and pulled away from Brian. *I've just been sleeping with a stranger!*

All Amy knew about this guy was that his name was Brian Something-or-other and that his family lived in NYC. To be so *familiar* with someone so quickly was not like her at all. What must this guy, Brian, think of her? Amy could only hope that he had fallen asleep before she had so he hadn't noticed she'd been snuggled up against him. Then she remembered the red wine.

Fat chance that he fell asleep first. I must have passed out from that wine.

Amy smoothed out her sweater and fluffed up her hair as Brian opened his eyes. He stretched and smiled at her.

"Feel better now?" he asked.

Amy made a face. "I'm so sorry I fell asleep on you," she said. "I never drink, which is why that little glass of wine really got to me."

"That's okay," said Brian. "I think you were just tired."

"I was exhausted," said Amy. Still, she was so embarrassed she wanted to get away from Brian for a few minutes. She must look a fright. She decided to freshen up. She unbuckled her seatbelt and reached down to grab her purse. "I'll be back in a minute," she said, although she had no idea why she was telling Brian this.

Why am I treating him like a boyfriend? He's definitely not the man for me. That New York Jets sweatshirt is hardly a uniform.

As she headed back to the lavatory, she saw Travis standing in the small space next to an emergency exit. Two attractive young women were with him. All three were sipping from plastic cups, which made Amy feel like she was crashing a private party. She smoothed her hair and straightened her sweater.

Travis motioned to her. "Come join us, Annie. The flight attendant said it's okay if we stand here for a while to stretch our legs."

Annie? He thinks my name is Annie?

The two women gave Amy the once over. It was obvious they didn't want to share Travis's attention with her. But what could they do?

"What time is it?" Amy asked. "How much longer till we get to New York?"

"It's nearly 2:00," said one of the girls. "We should be in New York soon."

"That's the good news," said Travis.

Amy gulped. "What do you mean? Is there bad news?" She looked around. "Is the plane all right?"

"The plane's fine," said Travis. "But they're expecting JFK to get snowed in soon. If we're lucky, we'll be able to land before they shut down the airport. If not, we'll be rerouted and have to land at another airport that has better weather."

Amy shuddered at the thought. "Close the airport? But what about connecting flights? We...I mean, I have to get to Kansas City for Christmas!"

Travis scrunched up his face. "That's the *real* bad news. You probably won't get out of JFK, at least not for a day or two."

Amy was horrified. "But I can't spend Christmas in an airport!"

Travis smiled. "Relax, Annie. You won't have to. You and Brittany and Katie here can come home with me to the farm for Christmas. Even if the roads are closed and we have to spend tonight in the airport, I'm sure they'll be open in the morning. We'll be at the farm in time for Christmas dinner tomorrow."

"My name's Amy," she corrected him but Travis didn't seem to notice. Amy found this mildly annoying but not annoying enough that it kept her from daydreaming. She could just picture a white Christmas in the country at a beautiful farm. There'd be rolling hills, of course. And a big, rambling farmhouse with a cozy fire. And Travis's family would love Amy instantly. She was sure of it! It was all so romantic. Her fortune was coming true after all. Being on this flight, getting snowed in at JFK; it was all fate at work.

But there was still just one little problem. Well, two *big* problems, actually...Brittany and Katie. Amy and Travis couldn't very well enjoy a romantic holiday together with Brittany and Katie tagging along behind them. Somehow, Amy would have to persuade Travis that these two girls would have a wonderful Christmas at the airport with all the other stranded travelers. She decided to go back to her seat and work out a plan for making this happen.

Brian had unbuckled his seatbelt and was just about to stand up. "Can I get out before you sit down? I want to clean up a little before we land."

Amy remained in the aisle. "Sure."

Brian moved out of his seat and Amy scooted past him to sit down. He opened the overhead bin and pulled out a small bag. "Back in a few minutes."

Take as long as you like. It doesn't matter to me, she thought though she didn't say that. Instead, she smiled sweetly at him.

While Brian was gone Amy developed her plan. It was simple really. Brian seemed like a nice guy. She was sure he'd agree to offer to take Brittany and Katie with him to his parents' house so they wouldn't be stuck at the airport for Christmas. And she could persuade the girls that going home in the city with Brian would be so much better than driving for hours in bad weather to an old farm that was miles away. She'd just need to talk to the girls out of earshot of Travis, of course. As soon as they got off the plane at JFK, she'd head to the ladies' room and suggest Brittany and Katie join her. That shouldn't be too difficult.

A few minutes later, Brian returned to his seat. He had replaced his New York Jets sweatshirt and jeans with a dark blue cashmere crewneck sweater and soft gray corduroy slacks. He looked more clean-shaven and his hair was a bit tamer than before. He even smelled different – spicy and masculine.

Amy stared at his transformation. *Wow! He cleaned up nice!* Then she thought of her fortune again. *But he's not in uniform, so he can't be the guy for me. He just can't be!*

Soon the captain announced their approach to JFK Airport.

The man in the window seat next to Brian was awake now. He, Amy, and Brian sat gazing out the little window at the winter wonderland that began to come into view below them. The closer they got to the ground, the thicker the snowfall seemed. Finally the plane touched down and a few minutes later it arrived at the gate. The captain let everyone know he had some bad news. The airport would be shutting down soon and there would be no connecting flights.

There was a collective groan throughout the cabin.

Amy looked at Brian. "Will your parents be waiting for you in the terminal?"

"No," said Brian. "I have a car. And I was wondering…"

Amy didn't let him finish. "Would your parents mind if you brought someone home with you… someone who would have to spend Christmas Day in the airport otherwise?"

Brian's face lite up. "I'm sure they'd be fine with a stranded traveler coming home with me. They wouldn't want anyone to be stuck in an airport for Christmas."

The plane had come to a complete stop now and people were standing up ready to disembark.

"Good. Come on, then," said Amy. "Let's not get stuck in our seats and end up being the last ones off."

Brian stood up with her. Amy pulled her coat from the overhead bin, grabbed her purse and carry-on bag and made her way into the aisle. Brian got his bag and followed her off the plane.

Once they were in the terminal, Amy spotted Travis. Brittany and Katie were with him, along with a parade of other girls.

Where did they come from, Amy wondered.

Brian noticed them, too. "Look at that guy. He's such a player."

Amy felt defensive. "Why do you say that?"

"Isn't it obvious?" asked Brian. "He loves being surrounded by admiring women. I doubt if he has a serious girlfriend, though. One woman is as good as another to guys like him. He probably can't even keep their names straight."

"Oh, please don't say that," Amy blurted out. "He's wearing a uniform!"

Brian frowned. "Huh?"

"Oh, never mind," said Amy. "You wouldn't understand."

"Probably not," said Brian. "And anyway, I need to go to baggage claim and get the bag I checked."

"But you'll be back...right?" said Amy. She couldn't let Brian leave the airport without Brittany and Katie.

"Sure," said Brian. "But you can come with me if you like."

Now why would I want to tag along? Besides, I've got things to do.

"I'll just wait here," she said.

Brian shrugged. "Okay. Just don't move or I won't be able to find you when I get back."

"I'll be right here," said Amy.

As soon as Brian was out of sight, Amy rushed over to Travis.

"Hi, Annie," he said. "Have you decided to go with us to the farm?" He pointed outside. "It's snowing too hard to get on the road right now but as soon as it slackens up a little, we'll be on our way."

"Good idea," said Amy. She didn't bother reminding him yet again that her name was Amy and not Annie. Brittany and Katie were headed for the gift shop. "I'll be right back, Travis."

She caught up to the girls just before they got to the shop. "Hi, Brittany," she said.

The girls laughed. "My name's Bethany, not Brittany," said one of the girls.

"And I'm Kathy, not Katie," said the other. "Travis can't seem to keep it straight."

Amy sighed. "And I'm Amy, not Annie."

They all giggled.

"Oh, well, at least we're not trying to marry the guy. We just want to have some fun together," said Bethany.

Amy recalled what Brian had said about Travis. 'One woman is probably as good as another to that guy. '

Oh, what does Brian know about anything anyway?

She remembered her plan. "Can I talk to you two for a minute?"

"Sure," said Kathy. "But we want to pick up a few things before we leave, so can we talk in the gift shop?"

Before she could answer, the girls went into the shop. Annie followed them. Since she'd be spending Christmas Day with Travis and his family, she'd pick up a small gift for his mom and an inexpensive, appropriate gift for Travis, too.

The shop was decorated for the holidays with colorful lights and tinsel, and a Christmas song was playing over the store's sound system. The shop was jammed with people. Most of them were grabbing candy bars, chips, cold drinks, and bottled water – stocking up now on snacks while the store still had plenty to choose from.

Amy spied a colorful little snow globe on a shelf. *Everyone loves snow globes. I'll get this for Travis's mother,* she thought.

Then she looked around for something for Travis. A shot glass with a scene of New York City etched on it seemed perfect. She paid for her purchases then looked around for Kathy and Bethany but they had disappeared amongst the crowd. After a few minutes she gave up searching for them and decided to wait outside the shop.

She could see Travis sitting at the bar in the restaurant next door. He wasn't alone. Three attentive young women sat with him.

Amy could hear Brian's words in her head again. 'He's such a player. '

"Hey, Amy!" Brian had reappeared with a large suitcase on wheels. "I found you!"

"You're back," she said. *And you remember my name.*

"Yeah," said Brian. "And it has stopped snowing, so we can get going now, if you're ready. But let's call your parents first. I can give them my parents' address and phone number, so they'll know where you'll be. I've already called my parents to let them know I'm bringing someone home with me. They can't wait to meet you, Amy."

Oh, my, thought Amy. *This is not working out according to plan. I haven't had a chance to talk to Kathy and Bethany yet.*

Amy looked at Brian.

He had a huge smile on his face. She knew it was because he thought she was the one going with him to his parents' house for Christmas.

She looked at Travis.

He was still sitting at the bar, surrounded by admiring women...women whose names he probably couldn't even remember.

My fortune must be wrong. I don't want a man who can't even remember my name. I don't want a guy like Travis.

She smiled at Brian. "And I can't wait to meet your parents. They're so kind to rescue me like this. I'd hate to spend Christmas Day here, in an airport."

"Well, now you'll be spending Christmas Day in Manhattan," said Brian. "Are you ready to go, or do you want to call your parents first?"

"Oh, my parents," said Amy, suddenly remembering them. "They'll be worried when they hear my flight was cancelled. They'll be happy I'm not spending Christmas Day in the airport, of course. But my mother will ask me a million questions about you and your parents, and I really don't know anything about you or your family. "

"Well, there's not much to tell," said Brian. "My parents live on Park Avenue in Manhattan. My dad is an architect and I'm an architect. Our firm is Percival International. My mother is an artist."

Amy's eyes widened. She couldn't believe what she was hearing.

"Whoa! Stop! Hold on! You said you were just coming home to visit your parents for Christmas, so don't you live and work in Italy?"

Brian laughed. "Yes, I do," he said. "Outside Venice. Our firm has a big project there that I'm working on for the next year or so."

So you'll be going back to Venice after the holidays. Just like me. Oh, how wonderful! But Amy just had to ask what was now the most important question.

"So you don't have a wife? A girlfriend?"

Brian shook his head. "Neither, I'm afraid. My girlfriend and I broke up over a year ago when I moved to Italy. I haven't dated much since then."

Oh, this would all be so perfect, thought Amy, *if it weren't for that one little bit in my fortune about the uniform. Why can't I let that go?*

Before Amy could think of anything else to ask Brian, his cellphone buzzed. He took it out of his pocket and looked at the screen.

"It's Dixon," he said. "He's here with the car. We'd better get going. We can call your parents from the road." Brian picked up Amy's carry-on then wheeled his suitcase along as she trailed after him.

A sleek black Mercedes town car was sitting outside at the curb. A man got out of it and carefully made his way up the snowy sidewalk towards them.

Amy gasped.

The man was dressed in a black jacket, white shirt and black tie, black pants, and a black cap.

"Is that a uniform?" she whispered to Brian.

Oh, my gosh! A chauffeur's uniform?

Brian chuckled. "Well, I never really thought about it before. But, yeah, I guess it is."

Dixon approached Amy. "Good evening, miss. The sidewalk is icy in spots. Better take my arm. I'll lead you to the car and come back for Mr. Percival."

Amy giggled as she thought of her fortune.

Dixon thinks he's only leading me to the car. But I know he's really leading me to romance.

She could just picture herself in this big, black town car driving up to the Percival's luxurious apartment on Park Avenue. And she could just picture Brian Percival becoming her boyfriend this Christmas.

It's fate, she thought. She and Brian were meant to be together. She was sure of it!

ESTATE OF THE HEART

Barbara Glover

I first heard the voice as I stepped out of the elevator. It stopped me dead in my tracks, getting me looks of frustration and irritation as the rest of my fellow riders stepped around me. I followed the deep, rich tenor that washed over me like melted chocolate to Gloria's office door. It tugged me forward and I pressed my ear to the door as it caressed me, holding me enthralled.

The secretary scowled at me as she made to move out from behind her computer. The door opening unexpectedly saved me and a pair of strong arms caught me as I tumbled into the room. Hazel, almond-shaped eyes looked into my surprised ones. The owner of the voice had a sun-browned complexion, jet-black, shoulder-length hair, square jaw, and broad shoulders. Rugged, not handsome, he smelled as delicious as he sounded.

"Well, this is delightful." I could hear the laughter in his voice. "Are you all right?" The smooth, deep chocolate dripped over me leaving me breathless. I could feel the cords in his arms move as he set me upright.

"I'll call," I heard him say, and was delighted, until I heard my friend, Gloria, answer. I stepped into the secretary's area and stared as he walked toward the elevator. I noticed that the suit was tailor-made, nipping in the waist, accentuating his broad shoulders.

At the elevator he pushed the button and stepped back. His head swung toward me and his eyes met mine, holding them, and I couldn't have looked away even if I had tried. My whole body tingled. With a nod, he disappeared into the elevator. My breath left my body in a whoosh and I turned, ignoring the secretary who sat shaking her head, and entered Gloria's office.

"Who was *that*?" I asked once the door was closed.

"Blake Parker, just in from places unknown," answered Gloria moving papers and files on her desk. "Blake is apparently putting roots down in Victoria and wants to see the Stapleton estate. Which reminds me...tomorrow at 10:00 a. m., will you meet him at the estate and give him a tour? It's the only time he can make it and I've double-booked."

"I know nothing about showing real estate," I replied. "That's why I'm a wedding and party planner."

She waved her hand in dismissal. "It isn't rocket science. The doors will be unlocked, show him the place and gush over it like you did the pictures. Let him roam on his own if he likes and meet him at the door when you leave. I just need someone to be there."

"Ok, I'll do it, but if you lose the sale, I'm not responsible." The idea of spending time listening to that voice was irresistible.

"Put your hair up, and wear something...well, else," Gloria said, evaluating me over her reading glasses. I looked down at the black silk skirt hugging my hips and the emerald green blouse I thought was a good choice as it drew out the green in my eyes and the highlights in my auburn hair, which served as a halo for my pale skin. I had learned long ago that looks were everything to Gloria but I could never afford to meet her standards.

"I'm going to the Victoria Hotel to finalize plans for the Christmas party and I need to know — one Christmas tree or two? The ballroom will easily accommodate two so that would be no problem. We did order two, remember? We had also decided on sugared fruit on crystal dainty tiers interwoven with maroon ribbon and red poinsettias for the table centerpieces. The stairs will be swathed in holly, and huge wreaths will dot the walls and doors. Minimal but fantastic."

Gloria tapped her bottom lip. "One tree, I think, and did we decide on decorations? Clear lights, ribbon, nothing gaudy? We have a string quartet to play, have we not? Oh, and make it white silk ribbon not maroon."

"The next couple months will go fast," I assured Gloria. This was the most anticipated event of the Christmas season for some people in Gloria's circle. This Christmas party was planned down to the most miniscule detail. The venue for next year was already decided upon and booked, the trees ordered in July, and the invitations would be back from the printers in early September, which meant that the guest list was made up in May and finalized in June. Nothing was left to chance. This was a soirée that said *Thank you, Merry Christmas,* and paid off favours to people who were essential to Gloria's success. It was also a way of showing everyone how successful Gloria was at selling real estate.

The sun shone, bright and cheery, the next morning when I drove up between manicured hedges to the estate. He was already there leaning against his Mercedes, legs and arms crossed. I pulled up beside him and the door opened quite unexpectedly. He was fast, I thought, taking the warm hand offered.

"Good morning, Miss Williams. Punctual, I see. Not a trait one often sees in women." His rich chocolate voice flowed over me.

I gave my head a shake to clear it. "That, Mr. Parker, is probably because you don't know many working women," I retorted.

"I stand corrected," he smiled, sounding amused. "I wasn't aware you were into real estate, although I do consider this a bonus."

"Gloria has been waylaid and asked me to stand in. Shall we go in, Mr. Parker?" I asked advancing toward the front doors.

"Please, call me Blake." He walked beside me with his hand on my lower back. The warmth felt intimate to me.

"This is the foyer...wow, that's one huge chandelier. Holy cow!" I exclaimed in admiration walking beneath it while straining my neck to look at the dancing coloured light refracting through the thousands of crystals. "The pictures certainly didn't do the place justice, did they?" I commented looking about me. "For instance, just look at this staircase. Four or five people could easily walk side by side up the stairs and not even touch. It would be perfect for wedding or anniversary or even family pictures. Have you ever seen anything like it?"

"No, I can't say that I have," was his response. When I looked at him, I realized that he wasn't looking at the crystals or the stairs. He was looking at me with an amused smile on his face. I felt heat rise in my cheeks.

"I'm sorry. I get carried away with beauty and structure that is on a grand scale. I've seen pictures of this house; however, I never thought I would actually see the real thing. It's marvellous. Shall we begin upstairs with the bedrooms? There are six, and each has its own ensuite and walk-in closet..."

"I think we should stay downstairs." His voice had developed a husky tone.

We viewed all the rooms on the main floor but when we came to the ballroom with all the glass walls and the black and white checked floor, I stopped in awe. It was a decorator's dream—or nightmare—depending on how you interpreted the space. I was already planning a masked Halloween ball with thousands of orange and white lights, fog drifting up from the floor and swirling around the guests' legs, or perhaps a chess or checker board with people as the game pieces. I sighed.

"Let's take a stroll outside those doors," I suggested, pointing to the French patio doors surrounded by white damask drapery hanging ceiling to floor. "They are supposed to lead to a gazebo and the gardens. I believe there is an all-terrain vehicle in the garage if you'd like to inspect the grounds farther afield."

He cleared his throat. "Fresh air would be nice at the moment. " When he took my arm, it tingled at his touch.

As we walked through a hedge, he slowed his steps to match mine. "Why do you love the house so much? You speak with delight about the beauty in this place; you see potential where others would only see a room. You have smiled continually from the moment you walked in the front doors. You're beautiful!"

I found it difficult to breathe standing so close to him. "Gloria is beautiful," I replied watching the slate walkway below my feet. "Not me."

His fingers raised my chin until I was looking at him. When he smiled, I thought my knees would buckle. "Botox is not beauty," he said. "Your beauty is warm, intoxicating. The two are miles apart." He bent his head and ran his lips lightly over mine. I stood stalk-still. Then he took my hand and planted a feather-light kiss in the palm, never taking his eyes from mine. Finally, still holding my hand, he said, "Let's explore these gardens. Who, may I ask, needs a hundred varieties of roses and who on earth looks after them all?"

"You do, and Peter does. He's the gardener," I replied breathlessly. "Hazel is the cook and Maria is the maid. They all have one-bedroom apartments in the basement and share a common kitchen."

"So in fact, I would own two kitchens if I bought the place. Gloria has misrepresented the specs."

"Oh no. Not intentionally, Mr. Parker, in fact..."

He laid a finger on my lips. "Call me Blake. It's difficult to begin a trusting relationship when one isn't on a first-name basis." We ambled through the rose garden as the sweet scent tickled my senses. He picked a rose and with a bow and handed it to me.

He glanced at a gold wristwatch. "Now, I must be off," he said. "If you're agreeable, I'll pick you up at seven for dinner. Nothing fancy but I know of a great burger joint and I'd love to take you there." All the way back to the car he held my hand then he opened the door assisted me in. Without a backward glance, he walked to his car, got in, and drove away.

It wasn't until later that I realized that he hadn't *asked* me to dinner. He had more or less told me I was going and I hadn't said no. It did seem odd to me that with all his money we were going to eat burgers.

After that we saw each other every evening for several weeks. We did everything from eat burgers at Burger Joe's to attend a ballet performance. We took a carriage ride through the park in the evening and went Christmas shopping together. When we decided to decorate our respective Christmas trees one day, we discovered that he had neither a tree nor decorations. So we shopped for those.

"You do know that fairy tales don't come true," Gloria said, laying a hand on my arm. "The princess doesn't always get her prince. I'm sorry, darling." We had finished discussing the last minute details for the Christmas party. "You need to come off of cloud nine and get back to reality. You and Blake are worlds apart. He's built up millions in companies and you are a party planner. When this honeymoon phase is over what will you talk about? What do you know of his businesses, and what does he care of yours?"

I felt like a fist had slammed into my stomach. *Can she be right?* When Blake and I went out that night, I kept asking myself, *Can this last?*

"I have to work tomorrow," I said to Blake after dinner. "My first client is at nine. "

"You've been quiet all evening. Is here anything you want to talk about?"

"No. I'm just tired. It's a busy season for me. "

"Maybe we should cut back from every night to every second night. I'm not sure I wouldn't be arrested for standing under your window though and throwing rocks until you opened up. I could have a violinist come and play you a nighttime lullaby. "

"In that case you better hope the rock hits the right window," I said as he opened the car door and then kissed me so thoroughly I was tingly in some spots and weak in others.

We drove to my apartment in comfortable silence. I was cocooned in the passenger seat and dozed in the warmth, comfort, and safety that Blake radiated. I didn't realize we had stopped until I felt I was being watched and I sat up to see Blake looking at me with an intent, almost hungry, expression on his face.

"I'll walk you to your door, sleeping beauty," was all he said.

At the door his arms came around me. "You smell divine," he said nibbling on my ear. I ran my hand through his hair. He kissed my throat and my knees melted. I leaned into him, clinging to him as a drowning woman would a life buoy. I heard him groan as his mouth devoured mine. Then he stepped back and took a deep breath. I felt light-headed. He held my shoulders to steady me then opened the door and pressed me, stumbling, through it. I heard him say softly, "I'll call."

The next day I survived, as usual, on coffee and daydreams. By the end of the day I was exhausted from checking my cell every fifteen minutes waiting for his text or call. By dinnertime, I realized he might not call. I curled up in the rocker feeling sorry for myself. When I finally went to bed the sun was rising.

Two weeks later I met with Gloria over lunch to add the finishing touches to the Christmas party. Halfway through our salads, talk turned to real estate — as always. "Thank you for showing Blake the estate. This is my thank-you, especially as he didn't quibble over the price." She pushed a white envelope across the table. "I would have given it to you sooner, however, I haven't seen much of you lately."

"He bought the estate?" I asked.

"Yes. Walked into the office the day after he had seen it and said the bank was ready to transfer the funds whenever I finalized the sale. I told him I'd have the papers ready by end of day; however, he said he had a plane to catch and his assistant would be in touch. I've sent the papers and all is finalized."

"He said nothing to me about buying the estate. Where was he going?"

"Like I would know," Gloria said.

"Did he say when he was returning?"

"No. I don't know where he's gone or when he'll return. I don't get involved in my clients' affairs. You would be the one with those details, I would think. He has other interests internationally. Why, he may even have a wife and kids?" Gloria said, unaware of how the words stung. Her comments made me realize just how little I knew of Blake and his life. For all the time we had spent together we hardly knew each other at all. I felt like my heart took a nosedive into my toes.

Weeks passed and I learned that a broken heart didn't mend, but the pain gradually eased. The anger turned from rage to smoldering coals of indignation. I constantly thought of Blake but after a while, I didn't feel like I was floundering.

One of my regular clients was hosting her annual masquerade Christmas party. Dressed as Queen Elizabeth I, I was inspecting the buffet table to make sure there was an ample supply of food when I heard the voice just down the table. My body tensed. Then that rich tenor washed over me and I almost dropped the plate I was holding. I felt the urge to run but my feet moved closer instead.

A musketeer. I should have known how well the costume would suit him with his dark colouring and long hair. The breeches accentuated his thighs and the coat nipped and tucked in all the right places. I wondered if he would still smell of spice. Would his lips still make me weak at the knees? I longed to find out so I put my mask in place and moved closer.

Blake was talking to a princess. He saw me watching and bowed low at the waist. "Your Majesty," he acknowledged me in the deep voice that set my skin on fire and took my breath away. Then he turned his attention once again to the princess. I walked away, eager to find fresh air. It seemed like Blake had materialized from wherever he had gone, and he didn't recognize me. Gloria had been right. I was nothing to him.

That night I received a text:

Chelsea, I arrived back today. I'll pick you up at 7 tomorrow for dinner. Text or call to confirm. I've missed you. I can hardly wait to see you again.

As much as I wanted to see him, I thought perhaps it was better to end it. Prolonging the agony would be devastating and I may not recover. The doorbell rang and I didn't answer. The phone rang and I had to sit listening to the sound of his voice on the answering machine. Flowers came to my door and I set them in my bedroom. A long stem rose arrived with chocolates and an invitation to dinner. The invitation sat on my desk beside the rose. I did not respond.

Gloria called in to see me a few days later. "Blake is back in town," she mentioned after the air kisses and we had settled at our table.

"I know," I replied. "He is out of my league, remember."

"I could have been wrong about that. After all there was Cinderella," Gloria said.

"Fairy tale. Doesn't apply," I responded.

"Hmm. Probably you're right," she said.

"He said he'd call. Just one text, one message telling me he couldn't, he cared, something, anything would have been preferable to the horrible silence that followed his leaving." I blurted out as tears filled my eyes. I was horrified that I had revealed all this to Gloria the one person who definitely would not understand.

"Oh sweetie. It's that bad, is it?" she asked, surprising me.

"I saw him at the masquerade party but I couldn't speak to him." And I told Gloria everything, letting it all out like I had never done before. "He didn't call. I waited, I sent texts, silence; all I got was silence. He was at the masquerade party. He went there first before he even called me. He sent flowers, a dinner invitation. I love him. " I tried to hold back the tears, amazed at what I had admitted. It was true. I did love him.

"I see," was all she said. "Have you tried to contact him since his return?"

"No. I was too angry then I was too hurt. Now it's too late. I'll be fine. I just need to get over this," I said sniffing and dabbing at my eyes. "This is a very busy time. I'll have as much time to think of him as he obviously had to think of me."

"I'll get us fresh tissues," she said and rose from her chair. I held out my hand when I detected movement beside me and something soft was placed in my hand. I looked at it and then up at Blake.

"Hi Chelsea," came the deep chocolate voice, smooth as silk. "How have you been?"

"Go away," I said, turning my back was to him. I looked a mess.

"Will it help if I apologize? Can I explain?"

"No, but you can get lost. That would be comforting."

"I'm sorry, Chelsea. This whole thing is my fault. I didn't handle things well, did I? Some developments in one of my companies arose and I had to straighten things out. If it weren't crucial I would have stayed but I've been working on this for four years. It would have put a greater part of my company at risk so I couldn't afford to ignore it. The company is people, Chelsea, people with families, and debt, with real-life problems. They need this project. Sometimes things are bigger than what we expect them to be. Can you understand that?"

"All the technology in the world and you couldn't have called?"

"I'm sorry."

"I think you've said enough. Please leave."

"I went to a masquerade party because I knew you organized it and would be there. The problem was that once there I had no idea who you would be dressed as and I could only hope I would pick you out or see you without the mask. I stood around the banquet table all night hoping to find you."

"You bowed to me with such flourish any queen would have been struck by your manners," I assured him, turning so I was in profile to him.

"You were the Elizabeth? Why didn't you say something? Why did I not see it?"

"Pride. Anger. You could have answered at least one of my texts."

"But I love you. I love you with all my heart."

The last three weeks before Christmas were like a dream. There was a hint of promise for our future in the air. We spent more time before the fireplace in the evening with wine and classic Christmas stories reading our favourites to each other. We skated through the days with the confidence of love.

One Saturday morning my girlfriend and I were sitting at our favourite spot, enjoying a latte and watching snowflakes fall, which were rare in Victoria. Suddenly, a movement across the street caught my attention. Blake and Gloria exited Chun's Jewellery, a store where there were no prices and if you had to ask then you obviously couldn't afford to shop there. I saw him lift her in the air and swing her around then set her feet on the pavement and bend to kiss her cheek. He then pulled her hand through his arm and they strode off down the street.

My world instantly became as though the needle skids across a vinyl record and comes to a dead stop.

Christmas was now only ten days away. Music filled the stores; people were hustling to finish their shopping. Everything glittered in silver and gold, in red and green. Yet all my joy had flown. I felt heavy and depressed, like everything was dark. I had been a fool. He could call, text, email, and camp outside my door for all I cared, the relationship was over. All I had to do was get through Gloria's Christmas party then I would leave for a few weeks' vacation. My bags were already packed.

When the party was in full swing I walked up the staircase to catch of glimpse of the crowd below. When I saw him, my stomach did a flip. He was looking up at me and as our eyes locked, he nodded his dark head and raised his glass in a toast. Feeling benevolent, I nodded in return. It was Christmas, no hard feelings.

Gloria came to stand beside me. "You look lovely in green, Chelsea. It's a colour you should wear more often. I don't suppose you know what it does to your eyes and complexion, do you?"

I stared at her. *A compliment from Gloria? On something I am wearing?* This was indeed the season of miracles.

"You've been very distant lately."

"I've replied to all of your messages, and I've been very busy. The party is going off without a hitch." I didn't want a conversation with her.

"I see Blake has arrived. Have you spoken to him?"

"Why would I? Is he planning a party in the near future?"

"Yes. I believe he may be but we'll have to see." Gloria smiled at me.

"I'll not be planning that party," I snapped as I spun away, walked down the stairs and out into the garden. Planning Blake and Gloria's wedding, reception and dance was more than I could even think of at the moment. I would never do it.

"Hi Chelsea. How have you been?" The timbre of his voice caressed me.

"I'm fine." I turned as I heard the crunch of gravel under foot trying to look nonchalant. My heart beat a staccato in my chest.

"I imagine I've bungled things again. You have been ignoring me. When do you plan to grow up?"

"Excuse me? Grow up? I would think perhaps you could use doing a little of that. What kind of sick person are you? No. I'm wrong. We have no commitment to each other so I'm out of line."

"What are you talking about?"

"You and Gloria. How long has that been going on? How long have you been seeing her, and exactly when have you had the time?"

"Gloria has nothing to do with this..."

"Yes, she does. I saw you. I saw both of you." I jabbed my finger at his chest with each word. "You were coming out of Chun's Jewelry and you picked her up and swung her around then kissed her. I think she has a lot to do with it." I was shaking with anger.

"I see," he said. "Perhaps we should sit down." He gestured toward the bench in the darkness. "We can talk this out, sweetie."

"I'm not your sweetie and I will not sit down." I turned and walked away from him.

"What you saw was Gloria helping me. I needed her advice" he called to my back. "I didn't think what it would look like to others."

I walked farther away and through the tears I realized that should I never see him again my heart would turn to dust. I did not want to walk away; I wanted to be wrapped in those strong arms to be loved.

"Are you so insecure over our relationship?" he asked quietly.

"What do you think? First, you disappear for a month with no word at all. Then I see you coming out of a jewelry store and kissing a woman who isn't me. Insecure? You bet I'm a little insecure."

"Then I suppose I had better do something about it."

"And what exactly would you do? Don't you think you've created enough hurt?" I turned toward him but couldn't see him in the dark. Then I realized he was on his knees. "What are you doing? Are you all right?"

"Just listen, Chelsea. When you saw Gloria and me at Chun's, she was doing me a favour. It never occurred to me what it would look like to someone else. Gloria was helping me buy something very special. I have a house I bought especially with you in mind. Please. . ."

"I know about the house. Gloria told me you bought it. Good for you, and for your information fifteen thousand square feet on umpteen dozen acres of land is not a house. It has six bedrooms and a ballroom, for heaven's sake. No normal person calls that a house."

"Chelsea, look at me. I'm down here on my knees, on stone, holding out a ring, I'm trying to propose to the one woman I love with all my heart, and you are giving me a lecture on the difference between a house and an estate. Seriously?"

I stood in silence gazing at his face. He loved me with all his heart; he had said it in word and deed. I had been a fool. I didn't need the estate or the ring; I needed him, and I knew it was now or never.

"Yes," I said, stepping forward, and as I did so my body began to thrum to a tune older than time. He rose to envelope me in his arms and as we kissed in the moonlight I had no doubt that I was loved and that this love would be forever.

BROWN SANTA

Wendy Dewar Hughes

CHAPTER ONE

By the time she arrived at the store and wheeled her SUV full of boxes into the side parking lot the rain had started. Not that rain at this time of year was anything unusual; in fact, rain in November in the Pacific Northwest was pretty much a given. She just wished it hadn't started so early today because it meant heaving boxes of stock from the car into the shop while trying to keep her hair from becoming glued to her head like a helmet.

Caroline Jepson hopped out of the car and ran to the front door of The Tufted Puffin to find that UPS had already been and gone, leaving a tag on the doorknob.

"Oh, for goodness sake!" she said, yanking the tag off. Now she would have to call them and arrange for another delivery. With everything else on her list today, she didn't need any more delays. The biggest wedding in town was taking place in a few days and with customers wanting gifts wrapped in her signature style, her to-do list had grown as long as a broom handle. New stock had arrived a few days earlier and with the back room packed to the rafters, Caroline had taken the boxes home to unpack and price before loading the stock into the boxes again and bringing them back to the shop. Now she had to find places for everything.

She twisted the key in the lock and ran to turn off the alarm then headed back out again. By the time she had all the boxes lugged in, the rain had become a downpour and her hair, usually nicely curved and fluffed, lay on her head like wet seaweed. The weather then progressed from dismal to downright wretched. The wind picked up and drove sheets of rain down the street as the gutters overflowed onto the sidewalk. *No need to worry about too many customers today*, she thought. *No one in her right mind would go shopping on a day like this.*

Just as Caroline hefted the last box through the front door, kicking it closed behind her, the telephone rang.

Plunking the carton down on top of another one, she ran for the phone.

"Caroline, it's Lisa," said the frail voice on the other end. "I'm so sorry but I can't come in to work today. I've been throwing up all night and my mom wants to come over and take me to the hospital."

"Oh, dear. Well, if your mom thinks you need to go to the hospital then you probably do. I'll be fine today without you. Look after yourself, sweetie, and get well."

Ringing off with a sigh, she thought, *Eight boxes of stock and no helper.*

By mid-afternoon, Caroline had gone through three entire boxes. One contained accessories such as scarves, jewelry, and sparkly hairclips to go with holiday outfits. The next one she tackled contained a line of goofy mugs, tea-for-one sets, and salt and pepper shakers. These items always sold well both in the summer and this time of year. Two hours later, she peered out the rain-slashed window into the gathering dusk. Only one customer had stopped by all day, and she had only spent $4.99 on a headband. Caroline was about to call it a day and close up early when the looming shape of the UPS truck came into view.

Since there was no other traffic on the street, she couldn't miss the fact that the truck was headed her way. It drew to a halt outside her door.

"Oh, no," she moaned. "Not more stock today. I'll be at this all night."

In a moment, the driver leapt from the truck and, ducking under the little awning, lunged through the front door.

"Man, what a day out there," said the tall uniformed man, setting a big box on the floor. "I wasn't going to come back this way but it was a light run today so I thought I'd give it one more try before going home."

"Thanks. . . I guess."

He grinned at her as he wiped water off his cheeks with his palms. "I've got one more for you. Hang on."

"Not going anywhere," she mumbled at his disappearing back.

Seconds later he was back with another equally enormous box. "That about does it. Sign here," he said, handing her the manifest.

"Hey," Caroline said, scribbling her name down, "I was thinking of closing up early but really can't. If you're done for the day, would you like to dry off for a few minutes and have a cup of tea? You're only the second person I've seen all day." She stuck out her hand and introduced herself.

"Joe Pomeroy," the driver said, "and I'll take you up on that." Caroline liked the way his brown eyes crinkled at the corners when he smiled at her. Dark wavy hair, shot through with silver, curled over his ears. "Heaving boxes around all day is tiring work for a guy my age." Caroline didn't think he looked that old, perhaps only a few years older than she, which meant hovering around the fifty mark.

"You must be new on this route," she commented over cups of Earl Grey. "I don't think I've seen you here before."

"I'm not only new to the route, I'm new to the job," Joe Pomeroy explained. "I retired but discovered that I could only play so many rounds of golf before getting either rained out or bored. I missed working everyday. It gives your life structure, don't you think?"

Caroline laughed. "Sometimes far too much. I feel like I live here when it's busy."

"Do you have a significant someone at home waiting for you?" he asked, surprising her with his forthrightness.

Caroline shook her head. "Not for a long time. It's a long, and not very pretty story but," she sat up straighter and brushed cookie crumbs from her lap, "that was then, and this is now. How about you?"

Joe didn't answer for a moment. "My wife, June, died of cancer two years ago. The kids, one daughter and two sons, are scattered around the country with their own lives. I moved here after I took early retirement because I always wanted to live near the sea and in a small town where I can get to know people without having to work with them."

"What did you do before getting into the brown uniform?"

"Astro-physics," Joe answered, "also known as rocket scientist. Thankfully, I don't have to be one to deliver packages to charming shops along Main Street now." He flashed an amiable smile at her. "I have discovered the need for a little physical fitness upgrade though. Heaving boxes is hard work but it's a lot less stressful than what I was doing before."

After the teapot had been drained, Caroline locked the front door and returned his wave as he drove away. *Nice*, she thought, and then began turning off the store lights.

The next day, Lisa's mother called only minutes after Caroline opened the shop to tell her that Lisa had gone in for an emergency appendectomy the previous evening and would be off work for at least three weeks. After she closed the shop that evening, Caroline picked up a huge bouquet of flowers and dropped by the hospital to see Lisa.

"I kind of left you in the lurch," Lisa said weakly, wincing as she turned toward Caroline. Her long blonde hair lay in a tangled mass on the pillow.

"No, you didn't," Caroline assured her. "Something will work out for the store. Your only job is to get better."

As Caroline walked back to her car, she pondered just how things could possibly work out. The big wedding gift order still required several hours' work and with stock coming daily now all she could foresee was plenty of late nights working alone to get things ready in time for the Christmas rush.

Rather than heading home, Caroline went through the drive-through at the local fast food restaurant and straight back to the shop. Letting herself in, she locked the door behind her and turned on the lights over the cash counter. There she munched down her burger and fries, then washed her hands and got to work. Fetching an armload of purchased gifts from the back room, she piled them on the counter. Several giftwrap designs and a rainbow of ribbons hung from rails and pegs behind her. She had just measured and cut a large sheet of paper in sea foam green with white sprigs scattered across it when she heard rapping on the front door.

Who could that be? She peered through the gloom of the shop but could see only a dark figure through the glass door. It wasn't unusual for a local person to drop in after hours if she was there, though she generally kept visits short if she had to work late. Leaving the paper and scissors on the counter, Caroline went to check.

Under the faint glow from the streetlight on the corner, Caroline saw that a man stood on the sidewalk, facing away from the door. Her heart skipped a beat. From the back she couldn't recognize him. Then he turned around and she recognized the kind brown eyes of the UPS driver who had shared tea and cookies with her the day before. At his feet sat a scruffy little brown dog. *What is he doing here?* she wondered.

Unlocking the door, she opened it just wide enough to stick her head out. "Still delivering at this hour?" she asked lightly.

Joe turned at the sound of her voice and laughed. "Goodness no. Comet and I thought we'd walk down this way for a change. He likes to go out on the pier when no one is around so he can sniff the air and bark at the gulls and nobody can complain. I saw the light on and wondered if everything was all right."

Caroline relaxed and opened the door a little wider. "It's fine except that my assistant ended up in the hospital and will be off work for the next few weeks. The Christmas shopping season is about to launch into full frenzy and I'm nowhere near prepared. That's why I'm still here."

"Is there any way I can help? I'm good at carrying boxes and Comet is a good watchdog though he mostly watches the insides of his eyelids."

Caroline laughed and glanced at the little dog that already looked bored and ready for a nap. "I could use help with unpacking stock and pricing everything but I wouldn't dream of asking you to help me. I'll get it done eventually."

"You're not asking me," Joe countered, "I'm offering. I could start right now if you like, unless you're uncomfortable being alone with me here. On second thought, you probably don't want a wandering ex-rocket scientist cum UPS driver hanging about. Comet and I will just leave you alone."

"No, wait," Caroline said. "If you're serious, I really could use the help. I don't know a soul who can stand in for Lisa and I'm in over my head with all the giftwrapping tonight. If you don't mind, that is."

"Done," Joe answered. "Comet has volunteered, too. Did you see him nod?" He tugged on the dog's leash so his head bobbed up and down. "See, he's in full agreement."

"Come on in then," Caroline said, pushing the door back and stepping aside. Flicking the lock in place behind Joe, she said, "The big boxes are in the back. If you don't mind dragging the first one out, I can get out the invoice and go over the prices. I have to get a lot of giftwrapping done tonight but there's room in front of the counter for you to work. I'll get you a chair. That way I can see what you unearth as you go."

"Sounds like a plan," Joe said, smiling like a kid at the fair. "Just point me in the right direction."

CHAPTER TWO

For the next six nights, Joe and his dog, Comet, showed up at the door of The Tufted Puffin to help Caroline process her new stock. He didn't have much flair for arranging things in the shop but was happy to take directions and do the heavy lifting.

"What would you say to a late dinner at The Cavern after this box is finished?" Joe asked as he pulled a glass figurine of leaping dolphins from foam packaging. "I think we deserve a break. My treat."

Caroline stopped moving a display of notepads to a new shelf and tilted her head at him. "Okay," she said, her voice edged with fatigue. "I'll just put this down; then we can leave the rest of that box until tomorrow."

The Cavern was one of only three restaurants in town that stayed open late and Caroline and Joe slid into a booth by the window in the dimly lit room.

"Hey, Jackie," Caroline said, greeting the server as she handed them both menus. "Any specials tonight?"

"Clam chowder is hot and so are the cheese and herb biscuits," Jackie, a tall brunette with a lazy southern accent, told her. "We also have Cajun penne and the Big Daddy burger on tonight."

Caroline looked across the table at Joe. "I think I'm up for the chowder," she said. "How about you?"

"Same," he replied, handing the menu back to Jackie, "and a coffee, black."

"Just water for me," Caroline said, answering the question in Jackie's eyes. "I don't need anything to interfere with my sleep tonight."

After the server left, Joe reached across the table and squeezed Caroline's hand. For a second, she thought of pulling it away but his touch felt so good. It had been a long time since a man had held her hand.

"You sure work hard," he said. "Do you ever take time off?"

Caroline shrugged. "I usually have Lisa look after the shop on Mondays because it's the quietest day. That way I can take Sunday and Monday off together but with her in the hospital, it doesn't look like I'll get an extra day for a while now. By the time she comes back, we'll be into the Christmas shopping days full tilt."

"Then you need to make your day off really count," Joe said, releasing her hand as Jackie set their meals before them.

Caroline flipped her napkin open on her lap. "Do you mind if we say grace? I like to thank God for the goodness in my life, and this sure smells good."

Joe smiled. "I don't mind at all."

A few minutes later, Caroline asked, "What did you mean, 'make your day off really count'? I usually spend it cleaning the house, doing my laundry, and cooking a meal that will last for the next few days."

"That sounds like a total blast," Joe commented, his eyes twinkling. "I'd hate to suggest you leave all those amusements behind to go flying with me."

Caroline choked on a bite of biscuit, coughing, eyes watering. "Do *what?*" she said once she caught her breath.

"I have a little plane over at the airport outside of town. I thought if you're interested, maybe we could take it up on Sunday afternoon, weather permitting. The forecast looks promising, so far, but it's a couple of days away. What do you say? Are you game?"

"I've never flown in a small plane before. Only the big ones that fly over oceans."

"This will be a bit different for you then. It's an open cockpit biplane, a two-seater."

"I guess we'll have to hope it's not raining."

"You mean you'll come?" he said, smiling broadly.

Caroline tugged on a strand of hair behind her ear. "It's hard to tear myself away from my laundry and housework but I can probably do it without incurring grievous injury."

Sunday dawned with cerulean blue, cloudless skies and no wind. After church, Caroline grabbed a quick tuna sandwich and an apple at her kitchen counter and went in search of warm clothes. Joe had instructed her to "bundle up." Once they reached higher altitudes it would be chilly in the open plane even if the sun happened to be out. She pulled out a parka that she kept in case of nasty winter weather — a pair of gloves, and a pale blue, mohair beret that she had purchased in Paris a decade before.

Standing before the hall mirror, she pulled the cap down over her ears and tucked some of her hair up inside it. After her husband, Andrew, had died suddenly from a brain aneurism, her mother had insisted that Caroline needed a vacation and took her to Paris for two weeks. It had been in March and still chilly so she had bought the hat at Galleries LaFayette and kept it ever since. It reminded her in a sweet, sad way of those days following her husband's death.

Caroline had met a few men since being single again but nothing had come of any of those first or second dates. After a while she gave up and decided if God wanted her to marry again, he would have to let her know. That's when she had bought the store and dived into her work.

When she heard the doorbell chime, Caroline slid the hat from her head and stuck it in the parka's pocket. Joe stood on the front step wearing aviator sunglasses and a leather flight jacket, complete with shearling lining and collar.

"Don't you look the epitome of the aeronaut," Caroline said, laughing.

"Wait until you see me in my helmet," Joe replied, producing a vintage leather flyer's helmet from his left pocket.

Twenty minutes later, Joe pulled his white pickup truck into the parking lot next to the county airport. "I came over earlier and rolled her out of the hangar so we wouldn't have to do it now. I've already filed my flight plan." He stopped the truck and turned off the engine. "There's my baby," he said, pointing to a bright little red biplane standing on the tarmac, glistening in the sunshine. "She's a beauty, isn't she?" he asked, gazing at the plane with immense fondness.

"I've never seen a cuter plane," she said. *Or a smaller one.* Pressing a hand to her stomach, she gave him a little smile and added, "I can hardly wait to fly in her."

"Come on, then," Joe said, leaping out of the pickup. Coming around to her side, he grabbed Caroline's hand and together they jogged to the little biplane. He instructed her how to get seated then climbed into the pilot's seat.

"It'll be noisy with the engine and the wind so we won't be able to talk once we get going," he told her, "but I can point things out and you might be able to read my lips." For a fleeting second, Caroline thought that she would like to do something with his lips other than read them but she pushed the thought away and concentrated on his instructions. "One of these days I'm going to get headsets but mostly I fly alone so I haven't needed them."

For a hiccup of time, that word "alone" hung between them. Then Joe removed his sunglasses and tugged on his leather helmet, complete with goggles, started the engine, and taxied out onto the runway. In what seemed like seconds, the ground dropped away and the plane skimmed over a hayfield and up above the pointed tops of the evergreens at the end of the runway. Banking left, the plane climbed into the blue and soon the water of the strait shimmered below, sparkling like a girl's party dress in the afternoon light.

Joe tapped Caroline's shoulder and pointed over the side of the plane. He shouted something but the words vanished into the wind. As they flew, he pointed out other landmarks, islands, towns and bridges. The earth lay below them like a jigsaw puzzle, its pieces scattered about the watery, dark blue table. Gleaming azure ponds punctuated dark patches of forest, strips of green meadows and yellowed hayfields. Ribbons of road and tufts of treed towns stitched the patchwork tableau together. Caroline could see the ferry powering across the strait, gleaming white against the blue and trailing a feathered wake. Her eyes watered from the wind and her hands and feet were numb from cold but she had not felt this exhilarated in a long time.

Until now, she had not realized that days and nights of practically living at the store, which left so little time for social anything, had narrowed her life into a long tunnel of all work and no play. Not since Joe Pomeroy came into her life had she felt so excited about living.

Every day she hoped he would stop by for a chat at the end of his shift or sit with her over cups of coffee or tea. Even though the wholesale shipping season had come to an end, except for a few back-order deliveries when no customers were around, she found herself drifting to the window of her shop and looking up the street for the brown delivery van.

Just a few days before, Joe had stopped by again with a small box for her shop.

"Hey, beautiful," he said as he bounded through the front door. "More presents for you."

"Oh, finally that back-order of Christmas napkins," Caroline said, reading the return address on the box and warming to the thought of his endearment.

"Just call me Brown Santa," Joe said, laughing. "I'm the guy in the brown uniform who comes bearing gifts. All I'm missing is the sleigh and eight tiny reindeer."

"You're short the big belly, a long, white beard, and your suit is brown, not red velvet," Caroline remarked. "However, as long as you keep bringing me gifts, you can wear brown if you want to."

She had signed his sheet, returned his good-bye wave, and watched him drive out of sight. An uncomfortably delicious feeling eddied through her mid-section. She realized that her heart had ticked up a notch with his appearance. *Could there be something happening in this relationship?* she wondered. Then shaking romantic thoughts from her head, she cut open the packaging and priced the napkins for display.

Still. Pulling open a file drawer she checked to see if any more back-orders were yet to arrive.

The racy red plane bumped along the tarmac as it came in for a landing and Caroline watched the propeller stop spinning as Joe cut the engine. Pulling off her hat, she shook out her hair and laughed, twisting in her seat to look at the pilot behind her.

"That's the most fun I've had all year," she said. "I'm freezing but that was a blast."

His face lit up. "You really liked it?"

"Oh, yes. Now, you're going to have to help me get out of this flying piece of origami because I can't feel my hands and feet." She pushed herself up as Joe leapt to the ground with ease and reached to help her down. Her slippery parka swooshed down the skin of the plane and she landed hard, knees buckling. Without hesitation, Joe caught her and lifted her back to her feet but held on as she clutched his shoulders.

"Whoa," he said. "I've got you." His face was so close to hers that she caught the faint scent of aftershave, something woodsy and she stopped moving. She wasn't certain her legs would hold her and it wasn't just because they were cold.

"Caroline, I..." He looked into her eyes. Slowly, his lips lowered to hers and his arms enveloped her. Her knees melted into water. He kissed her long and slowly then moved his mouth to a spot under her ear and dropped more kisses along the side of her jaw. Then his mouth found hers again and she savoured the sweetness of the sensations swirling through her. When he drew back a little, he placed his forehead against hers.

"I've wanted to do that for weeks," he whispered.

"Really?" Caroline said. "So it wasn't just me."

"No, baby," Joe said. "But as much as I'd love to stand out here kissing you, I have to put this plane in the hangar. Want to help?"

"Sure, flyboy," Caroline answered, smiling. "Then let's go get something to eat."

CHAPTER THREE

The days leading up to Christmas sped by in a tumult of shoppers, wrapping and special events at the store. Lisa had come back to work but could only handle four hours a day at most before she began to droop and make mistakes. Caroline sent her home every afternoon when customers started looking uncomfortable with her still-unwell condition. Every busy day meant an equally busy evening spent wrapping customers' gifts, re-arranging the store and keeping everything clean as the weather deteriorated into constant rain then slushy snow.

By mid-December, Joe started dropping by almost every day at closing time. Sometimes he brought food so he and Caroline could grab a quick dinner in the back room; other days he'd whisk her out to a nearby restaurant before she headed back to the shop. On Friday, Caroline kept the store open until nine o'clock and begged Lisa to come in and open in the morning, staying only until noon when Caroline took over and sent her home. Twelve days before Christmas, Lisa came down with the flu.

"I don't know what I'm going to do," Caroline moaned to Joe one evening as they sat in the back room while she checked invoices. "With Lisa off sick again, I'm going flat out. I'm not sure I can keep this up."

"There must be someone you could call. Any friends in town who might be able to step in, even for a few hours a day?"

Caroline shook her head. "I've already been through my list. Everyone is either too busy or going away. I guess I'll just have to keep putting one foot in front of the other until after the holidays."

"Don't get discouraged, sweetheart," Joe said. "It's only a dozen days until Christmas. Something might work out yet."

Caroline leaned into Joe's shoulder and he put his arm around her and drew her close. "I know we've only known each other for just over a month," she said, "but it feels like longer. You've been a good friend to me." She paused and nudged Comet's sleeping form with her toe. "You and Comet."

Joe leaned toward her and kissed her cheek. "Yeah, Comet always comes through," he said. Turning Caroline's face toward him with a fingertip under her chin, he said, "I will too, you know."

Just then the bell over the front door jingled and Caroline jumped to her feet. Joe's words jangled in her brain as she greeted the three women who entered the store. What did he mean, he would come through for her? In spite of her pre-occupation with work and the busiest season of the year, she couldn't deny that over the past few weeks she had been skidding down a slick slope. If it kept on like this, it was a slide that would end with her in his arms for good. She wasn't at all sure she was ready for that.

With only her half her mind engaged, she assisted her customers to find gifts and handled their purchases with a smile stitched in place on her face. Deeply aware that Joe sat at the little table on the other side of the wall at her back, she went through the motions and bid them good-bye when they left.

I have to get a grip on myself, she thought pressing a hand to her forehead. *This is no time to fall in love. I don't even have time to do my laundry. How will I fit a man into my life?*

"Hey," Joe's soft voice interrupted the monologue clattering through Caroline's tired brain. She startled and swung around, her hand to her throat. "Hey, hey," he repeated, reaching for her shoulder. "It's just me. Wow, you *are* wound up."

"Oh, Joe, I'm sorry. My mind was elsewhere."

"Listen," he said. "You take care. I have to go now but I'll be in touch, okay?"

Surprised at his abruptness, Caroline nodded and watched as he whistled for Comet then headed toward the door. "Okay," she said. "Will I see you tomorrow?"

"Maybe," he replied, pulling open the shop door and disappearing into the night.

For more than a minute, Caroline did nothing more than stare after him. *What just happened? Did I imagine it or did he suddenly change?* She pressed two fingertips to her right temple where a headache had suddenly flared. Had he actually said he would always come through for her or had she read something into his words that wasn't there? What did he mean anyway?

Glancing at the clock over the cash register, she went into the back room and dragged out the vacuum. She decided that the minute the clock struck six she was locking the door, cleaning up, and heading home.

As expected, the store got busier as each day brought Christmas closer. Caroline struggled to stay cheerful with her customers but she wasn't sleeping well. Joe had neither called nor stopped in since the night he had walked out with only a backward wave. Had it been something she'd said? Had she imagined that he was more invested in their growing relationship than he really was?

With only seven shopping days left until Christmas, Caroline stood before her bathroom mirror one morning and stared at the reflection of the woman looking back at her. Her usually vibrant mahogany hair hung in limp strands around her face and deep purple crescents underscored her eyes. She didn't look her age at all; she looked ten years older. Sighing, she stepped into the shower to begin the charade of being bright-eyed, perky and thrilled that it was nearly Christmas.

Half an hour later, thankful that it wasn't raining at least for now, Caroline turned the key in The Tufted Puffin's front door lock. She had just flicked on the lights in the shop and reached into the bowed display window to adjust a decoration on the miniature white Christmas tree when she glanced up the street.

She froze. Surely it couldn't be. Through the thin morning fog that cloaked the village street into soft focus she saw Joe standing on the next block. Instead of his brown UPS uniform he wore nice-fitting jeans and his leather flying jacket. Standing in the circle of his arms, leaning into his embrace, was a woman.

It was clear that they knew each other.

CHAPTER FOUR

Caroline gasped and pressed her back against the wall behind the shop door. So, this was why he had not been to see her nor called for days. A swallowed sob escaped her lips and tears blurred her vision.

Daring to take another look, she leaned into the window again. Sure enough, it was Joe. There was no mistaking the silver-sprinkled dark waves of his hair, and she would recognize that jacket anywhere. She tried to pull herself away from the sight but felt cemented to the spot as she watched him kiss the cheek of the other woman then sling an arm around her shoulders and walk up the street. When they had disappeared from view, she finally dragged her misted eyes away from where they had stood. Dabbing the tears with her fingertips, she sniffed loudly and straightened her blouse.

"I have to pull myself together," she ground out through clenched teeth to the angel figurine staring blandly at her from a nearby shelf. "I have a store to run."

The UPS truck didn't drive down her street once that day and by the end of the afternoon, Caroline had managed to convince herself that she had imagined a romance between herself and Joe all along, that the whole thing had been a construct of her imagination. Her emotions ping-ponged back and forth between feeling pathetic for having allowed herself to believe that he had cared for her, and feeling sure that he had meant it the numerous times he had kissed her. He had taken her for dinner, walked her home, and dropped by the store with lunches or fancy coffees. He had even taken her flying in his pride and joy — the biplane. What did it all mean?

By the time she started preparing to close the shop for the day, Caroline felt so drained she couldn't bring herself to do more that push the carpet sweeper over a few dirty spots, and flick the feather duster across a shelf or two. She picked up her coat and purse, turning off the back room light as she left the room. In two minutes, she would lock the door, cash out, and go home. She wasn't even hungry tonight. Draping her coat over the stool behind the counter, she set her purse on the floor at her feet and heard the bell over the front door jingle.

Groaning inwardly, she straightened up and tilted her head toward the front of the store. Her breath caught in her throat. Joe stepped through the door and under his arm was the woman Caroline had seen him kissing. She placed her palms down on the counter and drew in a long, slow breath.

"Hello, Joe," she said as evenly as she could muster.

Joe had a silly grin plastered across his face, like he had just launched a rocket and was immensely pleased with himself. "I have a surprise for you," he said.

Evidently, Caroline thought sourly, maintaining her plastic smile.

"I want you to meet Lana," Joe said, dropping his arm from where it had lain across the woman's shoulders. "She has agreed to come and help you."

Caroline looked at the woman standing before her smiling then dragged her stare back to Joe's ridiculously beaming face. "Excuse me?" was all she could say.

"I told you I would come through for you," he said. "I know you're having trouble keeping up with the Christmas rush, and I know how tired you are, so I went and got Lana to help you."

"I don't understand..."

"Oh, gosh," Lana said. "He's making a mess of this." She stuck out her hand to shake and Caroline gripped it lightly. "I'm Joe's sister. I had my own gift shop for twenty years and just sold it last summer. I know exactly what you're going through so when Joe called to see if I was free to come and help, I could hardly say no. I'd have been here sooner but my car broke down and he had to come and get me. Since I've been here Joe's been too busy with Christmas deliveries and every time we tried to come by, you had already closed the shop."

"I didn't want to call you at home in the evening," Joe added. "I know how tired you've been and frankly, I've been wiped myself by the end of the day."

"I'm a quick study, honestly," Lana said. "All I need you to do is show me how the cash works here and I can start first thing in the morning. I promise by tomorrow you'll be able to take the afternoon off."

All Caroline could think of to say was, "Okay. You're hired."

The remaining days before Christmas raced by as though they had been chased by a gale. Lana had shown up for work before Caroline had arrived the next day and stood waiting by the door for her to unlock it. It took no more than fifteen minutes to bring her up to speed on the workings of the shop. It was evident that Lana knew how to run a store, handle stock, treat customers and do fancy giftwrapping. Her energy seemed boundless.

On Lana's second day on the job, Joe stopped by to see how things were working out. Leaving Lana to attend to the front, Caroline led Joe into the backroom and gently closed the door.

"I don't know how to thank you," she began but he put a finger to her lips then replaced it with his own mouth, kissing her softly.

"You don't have to thank me," he said, holding her hands in his. "I couldn't stand watching you deteriorate into a puddle of fatigue everyday. I'm just sorry I didn't think of going for Lana sooner. We rocket scientist types aren't too swift sometimes."

Caroline laughed. "I have a feeling that Brown Santa is about to deliver the best Christmas ever."

JENNY BLUE EYES

Barbara Glover

The woman beside me in the crowded art gallery admonished her overactive son for the second time and for a moment he danced from foot to foot. Then he darted in front of me and she reached to grab him by the coat collar, catapulting me into the man at my left. The man's arms went tight about my waist to steady us both as I lurched hard against his chest.

Forgetting the wayward child, I became aware of the strength of this man's arms and the way his fingers pressed into my back. A wave of primitive desire swept through me like an ambush but I fought hard for control. I didn't realize I had leaned into him and now held onto the lapels of his coat with my face buried in his shoulder until I felt his arms loosen as he drew me up to face him. His eyes gazed into mine. "Did you feel that?" he asked, his voice raspy.

I nodded, agonisingly aware of how close he was, as every nerve in my body stood to attention. I stepped back, letting him go. "Thank you," I said in the most business-like tone I could muster.

That seemed to bring him back to reality and his gray eyes flickered and then shadowed as he took a deep breath and smiled. "I'm Brent Wilson," he said extending his hand.

Afraid to touch him and set off another electrical reaction, I said, "Thank you, Mr. Wilson." I backed away a couple of more steps knowing my face was flushed. I couldn't seem to take my eyes off of him. It was like there was an invisible thread connecting us. I couldn't seem to break it even knowing I was standing on dangerous ground. I saw his hand drop to his side.

I turned and rushed from the gallery, my heels clacking on the floor. Outside the cold air embraced me and I was grateful for its bolstering effect. As my head cleared, I called myself an idiot for letting silly fancies get the best of me. I drew in a deep breath of cold air. I had been made a fool of once in the name of love. I was determined it would not happen again.

That evening my girlfriend, Becky, and I met at La Blu for appetizers and a drink. She gushed about the art show and I nodded, stifling a yawn, and put my chin in my hand, elbow on the table. Her rambling could go on forever and I applied my own survival technique. I imagined that I was in a sophisticated restaurant and the tables were set for two with crisp white table clothes and napkins, gleaming silverware, spotless crystal and a rose at every table. A string quartet played soothingly in the background; the only lighting was candlelight. I was dressed in a silk maroon dress with a low V neckline and heels; my hair was swept up and pearls hung about my neck and ears. The only other occupant was a gentleman sitting at a distant table unable to take his gray eyes off of me. In my reverie, he smiled and lifted his wine glass in salute. Then my daydream shattered. I blinked and sat up straight, surprised. Those gray eyes belonged to Brent Wilson, and he was sitting at a table across the room. When he winked, I looked behind me to see who was there and saw no one. When I looked back he had turned back to his companions at the table.

I tried to pay closer attention to Becky's chatter and when I looked again at the table where Brent had been I was disappointed to find it was empty.

"May I have your business card?" said a voice at my elbow. I nearly jumped out of my seat.

I gaped at him. "I-I don't have one," I replied. He pulled a business card and pen from his inside suit pocket and handed them to me. "If you don't mind writing down your number, I'd like to call you." I just looked at it until Becky snatched both pen and card. "This is her cell, and this is her work. Please give her a call. I'd appreciate it," said Becky handing him back the pen and card.

"This is my business card," he said laying another one down beside my drink. I stopped glowering at Becky and looked up at him in time to see him tuck the business card with my numbers on it into his pocket. "Thank you, ladies," he said then nodded and walked away looking better than any man should in a tailored suit.

"What on earth did you do that for? He could be a stalker, a serial killer, or have a nasty gambling habit!" I snapped at Becky.

"I doubt it. I think he wants to get to know you. Who is he anyway?"

"His name is Brent Wilson and he works for a computer company," I said studying his business card. "He's probably a salesman. I bumped into him at the art gallery this afternoon."

"He seems nice. Are you going to call? Check him out?" Becky asked.

"No. I don't want any complications in my life," I said. "Shall we go? I have to work in the morning."

"You're kidding, right? It isn't every afternoon you meet Mr. Tall-and-Handsome in an art gallery, and it certainly isn't often he shows up at our table and asks for your number or gives you his card with all his info on it. Besides, how can something that good-looking be a complication?" asked Becky. "I know Simon broke your heart but you deserve to be happy. You are such a beautiful person. Sure, you got your heart broken once but not all men are that way. Give this man a chance and if he calls, say yes. Please say yes." Becky clasped her hands in front of her chest as if in prayer.

The week flew by. Christmas cloaked everyone in its atmosphere; the music, the smiling faces, the decorations; even the hustle and bustle was enjoyable. The lawyer I worked for had several court appearances during the week trying to clear his slate for Christmas holidays, so I was too busy to give a thought to anything other than work and shopping.

When my phone buzzed I was expecting confirmation from Becky for lunch.

Hello, Jenny blue eyes. I'd like to meet you for coffee. You name the time and place.

You owe me a drink for knocking me off my feet, but I'll be kind, my treat.

I dropped my phone into my handbag and went back to work. Soon it buzzed again.

Are you ignoring me? It's Christmas.

Have a heart. Meet me. Please?

Maybe it was time to move on but whenever I thought again of Simon I wanted all men to suffer. Simon and I had agreed to meet at a friend's weekend party when I saw him with his arm around a woman's waist whom I thought was his sister coming to visit for a week. I had been looking forward to meeting some of his family. I now shuddered at the thought. I had approached Simon and was about to slip my arm into his when he turned to me. The look on his face sent a chill through me. When he introduced me to his fiancé, he called me a close friend of his. I was shocked, stunned. I don't remember leaving the party but somehow I had. I cried for weeks after. I had given him one year of my life and I never knew about her. I felt as if a bullet had ripped through my heart.

Pushing all thoughts of Simon from my mind, I sent a reply to Brent.

I didn't knock you off your feet.

No thank you to meeting for coffee.

Stop texting me. I'm working.

Reply:

Jenny blue eyes. You're breaking my heart. Meet me once. You name the time, the place. Yes you did, but I'm not speaking literally.

I remembered the sensations that had run through my body at the gallery. I wondered if what I had felt was real. Surely a relationship couldn't be based on sensations felt at one meeting but still…

My name isn't Jenny, my eyes aren't blue.

No.

Reply:

Jennifer and Jen don't suit you.

Your eyes are as blue as the sky on a sunny cloudless day.

I received no more texts and spent the rest of the day arguing with myself about meeting him. I didn't want him touching me in case I wantonly fell into his arms.

Then again, I did want to fall wantonly into his arms and have him love me forever. *It is stupid to meet; he'll just let me down but what if he doesn't; what if it works, what if...* I gave my head a shake. I had knocked him off his feet. I smiled at the thought and tidied up my desk and office and checked my makeup. I let my black hair fall to my shoulders. I took my natural attractiveness for granted. I lifted my coat off the hook and left the office.

Outside, gentle snow was falling, muffling the noise of vehicles passing. The Santa at the end of the street shook his jingle bells calling attention to his charity. A man leaned against a car nearby, probably waiting for his wife to finish shopping. A taxi idled behind him. I decided to take the taxi. Tonight I wanted to be home and finish wrapping my gifts.

As I approached, the man leaning on the car ahead straightened. I assumed his wife must be behind me. Feeling a momentary pang of loneliness, I wondered, *What would it be like to have someone to wait while I shopped, or who shopped with me and helped me make those confusing purchase decisions?*

"Jenny blue eyes," said a deep voice. "May I take you home?" I stopped and looked at him. The snow had covered his tawny hair and I could see that his eyes had specks of green and gold in them. His mouth lifted in a lopsided grin. Almost before I knew what was happening he had the vehicle door open and I was seated in a warm leather seat.

"Tea?" He smiled as he put the car in gear and eased out into traffic. "It's been a long day and I could use a cup. Is there any place special you would like to go?" When I didn't answer, he continued. "I'll take you to my favourite spot; it isn't far. We'll have dinner and then I promise to drive you home."

"How did we get from taking me home to dinner?" I asked.

"It's 5:30. Aren't you even a little hungry? This place has a fabulous broccoli cheddar soup. I haven't been able to talk the chef out of the recipe yet but I'm working on him. This is a quaint little place I like." He pulled into a parking lot.

Once inside, he took my coat. "I'm glad you changed your mind and came with me," he whispered close to my ear, his breath stirring the hair on my neck and sending shivers down my spine. "So why were you at the gallery? Are you into art?"

"My friend Becky is the curator of the gallery. And you? Were you looking to buy some art?"

"No offence to Becky but I didn't really get the show at all. I like art to show me something — a house, a flower, people, animals — anything but lines. It wasn't my kind of thing at all," he said.

"Then why did you go?"

"Ever have a day when you need to be alone, someplace quiet? That's what I needed. I find I never see anyone I know at the art gallery and no one there ever talks above a whisper. It's the perfect thinking spot."

As he kept the conversation upbeat, I relaxed. Brent was obviously an extravert and I was laughing and enjoying myself — something that hadn't happened since Simon. Brent came from a family of four boys. "Mom stayed at home but then she pretty much had to, to keep tabs on the four of us. We learned early in the game, with mom around, there was no running amok. Dad, however, was the absent-minded professor. There were times I doubted he knew he had kids. I was always interested in computers so that was the direction for me. What about you?"

"I have one brother, one sister, one mother, one father. I gravitated toward administrative work. I like the people. I love the job. There isn't much else to tell."

"Why were you hesitant to give me your number?" he asked.

"You could have been a stalker, serial killer, all sorts of things," I said.

"Hmm. Good points, all of them but childhood and teen years aside, I'm a solid citizen. I vote, pay taxes, and try to be a decent human being." He traced a pattern in the napkin with a fingertip. "I can't forget what happened at the gallery. It was intense, surprising, and nothing I've ever felt before." He reached across the table to touch my hand but I snatched it away and laid it in my lap. He smiled. "We could be soul mates, who knows?"

I laughed. "I don't want to talk about it."

"You can't deny the lightning bolt and I'm sure you felt it, too. Are you not in the least bit curious what that was about?"

"It was chemistry and hormones, nothing more," I said. "Look, I don't deny that something happened but I learned not to trust that dance over a year ago. So I'm letting you know, nothing is going to happen between us."

"Really? I would like the chance to prove you wrong..."

Abruptly, I stood up. "I'm sorry, I can't do this and I don't want to do it," I said but part of me wished he could prove me wrong.

Outside there were no cabs to be seen. Brent caught my arm. "You can't go out without your coat. You'll catch cold." I twisted out of his grasp as I grabbed my coat from him. My fingers brushed his and I felt the energy tingle down my arm. His hand connected with my back and steered me toward his car.

"I'll take you home," he said. "I'm going to call you in a couple of days. It will give you some time to think about what we could have." Before I could slide into the seat, he caught me in his arms and kissed me softly. Then he let me go. "See? It's more than chemistry and hormones."

My head spun and I didn't know what to think. All I knew was that sitting here I was too close to him and that there was no denying the attraction I felt.

For the next several days, I kept myself busy and kept my phone turned off. The memory of his kiss and his touch kept running through my mind. Then I would think of Simon and give myself a reality check. Even

Becky became frustrated with me. "You're an idiot, Jenny. He's a good guy. Get to know him, give yourselves a chance. Not everyone is like Simon and you can't keep yourself in a bubble or before you know it you'll be having a mid-life crisis and all those 'what if's' in life will slap you up the back of your head so hard you'll flip out of your rocking chair."

A week and a half went by, then two. I finished my Christmas shopping and made plans to go home for Christmas. I spent my time off wandering around stores soaking in the Christmas Spirit.

Oddly, a couple of times a week, there Brent would be, getting a coffee in the same coffee shop, browsing magazines at the kiosk. Once in the bookstore he was going up the escalator as I was going down. I told Becky, "I go from not knowing he exists to seeing him everywhere."

"Does it creep you out?"

"No. Odd isn't it? I'm actually at the point where I look for him."

"Next time, buy him a coffee and offer it to him as he comes in the store. He's letting you know he's interested. For heaven's sake, talk to him."

"Your coffee, Mr. Wilson." I had spent the previous two days buying an extra coffee in case he showed up at my favourite coffee place. His eyebrows shot up but he smiled and accepted the cup. "I have to be at work in fifteen minutes," I continued, "so you can walk me there." I took his arm and led him out of the shop and down the street.

"This is a nice change," he said. "May I ask what has brought it on?"

"People were beginning to think you were a stalker. I'm trying to save your reputation."

"A sense of humour—I like that in a woman. What else should I be aware of?" He took a sip of his coffee

"The people on the floor of our office building are going carolling this evening. Can you sing?"

"Well, it has been some time but I'm willing to give it a try."

"Ok, meet me at the office at six. Third floor, turn left out of the elevator, 3rd door on the right," I said letting his arm go as I opened the door to my office building and left him standing on the icy sidewalk.

Brent showed up to go carolling with me, and with his extroverted personality, he fit in perfectly. After that we saw each other every few evenings for dinner, a movie, or just a quiet time watching TV. Every once in a while, I caught Brent gazing at me with a hungry look in his eyes but other than a kiss goodnight, which always felt controlled, he never tried anything further. At first I felt wary but eventually I relaxed knowing he was content to let the relationship find its way. I was happy; we got along well, and enjoyed long conversations on every topic under the sun. We decorated Brent's tree then sat in the dark watching the lights twinkle and drinking eggnog. I was the happiest I had been in a long time but I sometimes wondered if Brent wasn't content. I was too afraid to ask. I didn't want this to be over.

"Are we having dinner at my apartment? Spaghetti and meatballs are on the menu," I asked over the phone when he called.

"Sounds great. I have to work until six but I'll drop by when I'm done." He sounded sad.

He came in sometime later, rubbing his hands together. "The temperature is dropping. Man, that's cold."

We ate by candlelight, cozy and warm, but he was distant. Finally he said, "Jenny. I can't do this anymore." Brent put his fork down. "I want more from our relationship and you seem content with a few chaste kisses. I've tried to be patient but this isn't all I want."

"What do you mean?"

"Look at us—candles and flowers on the table, we shop together, cook together, do everything together but we don't do anything about us. I honestly cannot do it any longer." He stood up and got his coat and scarf. "I'm sorry. I love being close to you. In fact, I love you, which is why this relationship is impossible for me. I want more for both of us but as soon as I touch you, you shrink. I really hate this Simon guy. I hate what he's done to you because he's done it to both of us. I love you Jenny, and I want you in my life, but not like this. I want a real relationship." He ran his knuckle down the side of my cheek and then he was gone, the door closing so quietly I hardly heard it.

I picked up the half-eaten plates of food and dumped them, plates and all, in the garbage. He'd be back. Things would be just fine, I told myself. He loved me; he'd said so.

"You don't just walk away from someone you love," I said out load but all the time in my heart I knew he might not be back. What if it was over, if we were over? I sat on the couch, my body sagging in bitter disappointment, and watched the darkness steal across the room and slide over empty the furniture.

At four in the morning, I called Becky.

"Now would be the time for a cat, I suppose," she said.

"Becky, I want you to help solve this problem. Suggesting I get a cat isn't helping."

"You have to solve it yourself and you know the answer. It's 4:00 a.m. and you're talking to me on the phone. Do you not see what's wrong with this picture? You screwed up, admit it—only admit it to him, not to me." There was silence for a few moments then she added, "Man, you are a lot of work. Tomorrow is Friday. Pack a bag. Let's you and me spend the last weekend before Christmas at the resort. It'll be fun; skiing, hot tub, massages—we'll spoil ourselves for the weekend. We'll talk and you can decide what to do after Christmas. Agreed?"

"Agreed," I answered but my heart was not in it.

When Becky and I started our road trip, it was dark as it could be only in December. The forecast called for clear and sunny weather for the weekend, so we played CDs, sang Christmas carols, and reminisced about Christmases past. I put the dark and lonely feelings behind me, and Becky was as perky as always. The snowy road was devoid of traffic. Suddenly a large dark shape loomed in front of the car and I slammed on the brakes. There was a thud, a crash, and the sound of breaking glass then nothing.

When I opened my eyes I sensed a soft light coming from somewhere around me. Was I dead? Was this heaven? Slowly, blurred images passed before my eyes, and I knew I wasn't dead because when I turned my head it felt like a bomb had detonated inside it. My chest burned and I struggled to breathe. Nothing was familiar. The window curtains were drawn and it hurt to even think so I closed my eyes.

"I'm relieved you're awake." My eyes popped open at the sound of his voice. "I was worried about you." He sounded tired. I could feel his hand as it gently touched mine. He uncurled my fingers and made tiny circles in the centre of my palm with his fingertip.

"What happened?" I whispered, my throat dry.

"Here, have a sip of water." He held a straw to my lips. "You ran into a moose. It's done some serious damage to your vehicle but both you and Becky will be okay."

"Becky?"

"Becky is at home with two very sore knees and a big headache. You two came away pretty much unscathed. It could have been much worse."

"I would like to go home," I said, making small movements to get out of bed.

"You will be staying here until the doctor says you can leave. Tomorrow, he says. They want to observe you overnight. Your air bag didn't engage and they think you hit the steering wheel. X-rays show no damage. They have given me a chair, a blanket, and a pillow so I won't be far if you need anything."

"You can't stay."

"Apparently, I can. I told them you had no family near and I am your boyfriend. They were very sympathetic," he said.

I was too tired to argue and vaguely wondered how he found out about me, and the accident, but it hurt to think so I closed my eyes. When I woke during the night he was sprawled in the chair looking uncomfortable but asleep. I watched him; his dark lashes fringing his closed eyes, the peaceful look on his face, the long elegant fingers, a well and fit body. I felt touched that he had stayed but then sleep overtook me.

The next morning he took me home and made me tea while I crawled into bed. I had an excruciating headache and the tablets he gave me put me to sleep immediately. I awoke to rays of sunlight poking through the curtains. Sensing or knowing I had awakened, Brent appeared with a tray of soup and a photo album.

"I've been amusing myself looking through your photos. You were a very cute baby and then there was the gangly pupa age and then what a beauty emerged from the cocoon. Eat your soup, you need your strength," he said.

"What are you doing snooping through my things?" I reached out to grasp the album but a sharp pain filled my head and I sank back.

"Well, I'm not good at housekeeping, TV was boring, the stereo doesn't work...well, it didn't but I fixed it. You need a new one. So when I saw the albums I indulged myself then I made soup, looked at more pictures, and finally you woke up, which is good because I was getting bored."

"You've been here all day?"

"Yes. Eat up. My speciality is heating tins of soup. I will be insulted if you don't eat."

I smiled trying to imagine this large man in my tiny galley kitchen.

"She smiles," he said leaning over and brushing my lips with his.

I joined him in the living room later and we watched television and talked, sharing our stories.

"Let's watch the snow fall," he said, pulling the love seat in front of the window and opening the curtain. "The advantage of living on the twenty-fifth floor has to be the view." So we sat watching the snow falling outside, each of us tucked beneath a quilt, and with Christmas music playing softly in the background.

"We could see how far this could go," I said softly, so softly I wasn't sure he would hear. He was silent for a long time and I assumed he hadn't heard until I felt his hand touch mine as he laced his fingers through mine. He didn't even look at me but I could see him smile in the semi-dark.

"I'm already looking forward to this Christmas, Jenny blue eyes. What would you like to do when you're better?"

"Take a walk through the park in the dark, drive to a residential area and check out the lights on houses, shop only in stores that have a Christmas tree, go carolling, you?"

"Kiss you under the mistletoe, go for a sleigh ride and drink mulled cider, spend quiet evenings listening to Christmas music and discussing our future, shop only in stores that play Christmas music, visit a care home and take presents," he said.

I rose slowly and awkwardly, still stiff and sore, and looked out the window at the falling snow. It was so peaceful. I felt like a bird poised for flight. Now that the words had been spoken and the commitment made I felt unsure. I heard him come to me, felt his arms wrap around me and clasp lightly in front of my stomach, his head rested against mine. "We have all the time in the world to learn about each other," he whispered in my ear. I smiled and relaxed, leaning against his strength. "Merry Christmas, Jenny blue eyes," he whispered.

A CHRISTMAS KISS

Suzanne Lieurance

Sarah Langley had been working at Worthington, Kent and Associates in southern Florida as Charles Worthington's executive assistant for over three years. She loved her job—mainly because she was secretly in love with Mr. Worthington. Secretly, because even though he was single—he didn't have a girlfriend, as far as Sarah knew—Mr. Worthington was a firm believer in keeping business and pleasure separate. He went so far as to ban dating, or any other kind of personal relationships, amongst those who worked at the firm. Realistically, this meant Sarah had no hopes of ever having Mr. Worthington return her affections as long as she worked at Worthington, Kent and Associates. And since she didn't want to quit her job, she tried to convince herself she could be content just to see Mr. Worthington every weekday and earn his trust, respect, and appreciation for her hard work.

One morning in early December, Mr. Worthington appeared at Sarah's office with something that made her wonder — and hope — that his feelings for her, and his ban on personal relationships among employees, had changed.

"This is for you, Ms. Langley."

He shoved a small gift at Sarah. It was wrapped in gold foil with a huge red bow.

She took the gift from him and stared at it for a few moments. "What? For me?"

Mr. Worthington stood there, as handsome as ever in a smart gray suit with gray and white striped shirt and dark blue tie. Momentarily distracted from the gift by his thick, shiny brown hair that made her want to run her fingers through it, it took her a few moments to realize he was waiting for her to unwrap the gift.

"Oh...I can't imagine what this could be." She squealed with delight as she pulled off the red bow and set it on her desk and then carefully removed the gold paper to reveal a box with a cellophane window that allowed Sarah to see a huge Hershey's Kiss® inside. She took the kiss out of the box and examined it. The little white strip of paper streaming out of the huge chunk of candy said, "A Kiss for You!"

Now Sarah was even more confused — and more hopeful. Was Mr. Worthington trying to tell her something? Was she more to him than an executive assistant after all? Her heart fluttered. She looked at Mr. Worthington again with eager anticipation.

He rolled his deep brown eyes and said, "It's a reminder, Ms. Langley, of the K. I. S. S. principle."

Sarah didn't know what he was talking about but the word "kiss" made her think of love and romance. Her pulse raced.

Mr. Worthington frowned and said, "You do know the K. I. S. S. principle, don't you, Ms. Langley?" When she didn't respond he said, "Keep It Simple…uh… Sarah. K-I-S-S?"

Sarah's eyes widened and she quickly dropped the giant kiss onto her desk as if it were hot and had burned her hands. She felt faint. She remembered the K. I. S. S. principle now. And it definitely was *not* romantic. Plus, she knew the letters k-i-s-s didn't stand for Keep It Simple, Sarah. They stood for Keep It Simple, Stupid.

But, of course, Mr. Worthington would never call Sarah, or anyone else for that matter, stupid. He just wasn't that kind of man. But was he thinking it?

"You tend to complicate things a bit, Ms. Langley. Especially this time of year with holiday parties, vacations, and such, so this is just meant as a reminder. That's all." He turned to leave the office.

Sarah fought back tears. "Thank you, Mr. Worthington," was all she could think to say.

Once Mr. Worthington was out of sight, Margo, the receptionist for the firm, and the biggest gossip in the company, poked her head into Sarah's office. Her orangey red hair was pulled back in a ponytail at the top of her head and a pencil was laced through it like a chopstick. "You okay, Sarah? It's not like Mr. Worthington to come to your office, so I hope nothing's wrong."

Sarah wiped her eyes. She didn't quite know how to answer that question. Not that she *needed* to answer that question. It was none of Margo's business, after all. Still, if she didn't put Margo's mind to rest, Sarah knew all sorts of rumors would start to float through the office. And Sarah definitely didn't want that. Besides, nothing was wrong... exactly. Nothing except that now she knew for sure Mr. Worthington was *not* in love with her, and apparently he was also less than pleased with the way she managed things.

She thought she'd given up on winning Mr. Worthington's heart long ago and now she realized she'd only been kidding herself. But no wonder he wasn't in love with *her*. She had to admit that what Mr. Worthington said was true. She did tend to go overboard from time to time. Like that birthday party she was asked to plan for Mr. Worthington's six-year-old nephew when he was visiting with his mother last year. Sarah had hired a small circus to perform in the firm's parking lot. The child and his mother had been absolutely delighted with the party, but Mr. Worthington had raised an eyebrow when he saw the baby elephant...and the monkey. "I was thinking of something along the lines of lunch at Chester Cheese," he told Sarah later, "not circus animals pooping in our parking lot."

Sarah had smiled sheepishly and put the contact information for Chester Cheese in her Rolodex, just in case she was ever asked to plan another child's birthday party for Mr. Worthington, which she knew was unlikely.

Now she looked up at Margo. "Everything's fine. Mr. Worthington just needed to tell me something."

Margo eyed the gold foil, red bow, and the giant Hershey's Kiss® on the desk. From the looks of things, Mr. Worthington had come here for more than just talk, and Margo knew exactly what she'd tell everyone in the break room today. It would be the truth, too. "That's nice," she said to Sarah. "See you later then."

At noon, Mr. Worthington buzzed Sarah on the intercom. He wanted lunch.

Sarah went back to her old habits and immediately thought about how nice it would be if she popped round to Romano's Italian Restaurant on the corner and picked up a sampling of pasta dishes, salads, and breads for Mr. Worthington. Surely, if she continued to put such thought and care into everything she did for him, eventually he'd come to his senses and realize she was the woman for him. Then she happened to glance at the huge chocolate kiss on her bookcase and thought better of it. "Keep it simple, Sarah," she reminded herself. She decided to order Mr. Worthington a sandwich from Jimmy John's and have it delivered.

Around 1:30 that afternoon, Mr. Worthington called Sarah into his office.

"It's time to get a Christmas tree for the lobby," he told her. "But don't go overboard with the decorator this year, Ms. Langley." He looked at her sternly and tapped his long fingers on his desk. "No flocked tree with a million shiny ornaments and no little train and Santa's workshop. Just something simple but festive, okay?"

Sarah smiled weakly. "Right, Mr. Worthington," she said, but she noticed a sinking feeling in her stomach. Every year she looked forward to working with the firm's decorator to plan the perfect Christmas tree with the perfect lights and the perfect decorations. But this year, planning a "festive yet simple" tree didn't sound like much fun at all.

Sarah was sitting at her desk, poring through holiday issues of decorating magazines for some ideas, when Mr. Kent stopped by. He was the only partner in the firm who actually dropped in just to visit with Sarah from time to time. He was also the only partner who called her by her first name when the other partners weren't around. He had asked her to call him Brad, but Sarah never could bring herself to do that. She liked to keep things formal at work.

"Hi, Sarah. You busy?"

Sarah looked up from the magazines. "Oh...hello, Mr. Kent. I'm just trying to get some ideas for the company Christmas tree."

Mr. Kent came over to Sarah's desk and studied the pictures in the magazines. "You always do a great job with the tree," he said. His blue eyes sparkled and his crisp white shirtsleeves were rolled up to the elbow. "I'm sure you'll come up with something fantastic, like you always do. You turn the lobby into a holiday wonderland every year!"

Sarah smiled. "Thank you, Mr. Kent. That's kind of you to say, but Mr. Worthington wants something simple this year."

Mr. Kent didn't seem to hear her. He had spotted the chocolate kiss. "Hmmm...sweets for the sweet I see. Secret admirer?"

Sarah frowned. "Hardly. Mr. Worthington gave it to me."

Mr. Kent raised his eyebrows.

"Nothing like that," Sarah was quick to assure him. "It's meant to be a reminder of the K. I. S. S. principle, that's all."

Mr. Kent chuckled. "Oh, yeah, the K. I. S. S. principle. Charlie's on this 'simple but festive' kick right now." Mr.

Kent turned and looked out the window for a few seconds, as if he were giving the matter serious thought. "I know. How about a tree that reflects life here in Florida?"

"What do you mean?" asked Sarah.

"Well, to some people, traditional Christmas trees covered with decorations and tinsel always seem out of place here since it can be 80° at Christmas. So how about something more natural for Florida? How about a big palm tree with strings of colored lights?"

That sounded simple all right. But festive and elegant, too, if done well. Sarah immediately envisioned a Royal Palm in a giant gold pot. "That sounds perfect!" she said, "Thank you, Mr. Kent. I can always count on you when I need help. In fact, I almost feel like you're my big brother."

Mr. Kent's face suddenly went blank, which made Sarah wonder if she'd said the wrong thing. Had she actually managed to disappoint *two* of the partners at Worthington, Kent and Associates in a single day? Couldn't she do anything right anymore, she wondered.

"Well, I need to get back to work," Mr. Kent said finally. "See you later, Sarah."

When Mr. Kent had gone, Sarah immediately called the decorator and ordered a huge Royal Palm in a gilded pot. She asked the decorator to string the tree with lots of colorful lights, and an assortment of wrapped packages should surround the tree to make it look more like a Christmas tree. The decorator loved this idea and said she'd get right on it.

Later that afternoon, when the secretaries and paralegals were in the break room having coffee, Sarah stopped in for a soda. The minute Sarah entered the room Margo whispered something to Debbie, one of the paralegals. Debbie looked at Sarah and giggled. Sarah knew they were gossiping about her and Mr. Worthington. Had Margo heard what he had said to Sarah this morning? If so, soon everyone at the firm would know how disappointed Mr. Worthington was with Sarah. She trudged back to her office feeling worse than ever.

A few days later the potted Royal Palm arrived, along with the decorator who immediately went to work making sure the tree was set in just the right place, strung with just the right number of lights, and had just the right number of colorful gifts placed beneath it.

"It's magical!" said Sarah, even though she felt a few of her personal touches would have made it even better.

"Good job, Ms. Langley," said Mr. Worthington when he saw the tree. "Simple, yet festive. For once, you've given me exactly what I wanted."

Sarah beamed. She might not have Mr. Worthington's love yet, but she had managed to win his approval. It was a step in the right direction.

"Now I have another job for you, Ms. Langley," said Mr. Worthington. "Come with me to my office."

Once they were in Mr. Worthington's office, Sarah sat down in the chair across from him. She pulled a small notebook from her pocket.

"The office Christmas party is next on our list," he said. "As always, the partners and I like to have the party here during the day on the 23rd and then let people leave early for the holidays."

"Of course," said Sarah. She scribbled – *December 23rd, office party* – in her notebook and looked up at Mr. Worthington.

"But this year, remember to keep it simple, Ms. Langley." He paused to let his words sink in. "That means no waiters dressed as elves serving flaming canapés, no giant snowman cakes, no artificial

---

snowflakes floating down from the ceiling, and most importantly, no elaborate gift exchange. Do I make myself clear, Ms. Langley?"

Sarah could feel her face turn red as she remembered last year's Christmas party. "Right," Mr. Worthington. "Simple and festive," and she scribbled down the words as a reminder. "Got it. "

"Excellent. That is all, Ms. Langley."

Sarah spent most of the next few days trying to come up with a plan for the office Christmas party. But she couldn't help herself. Every plan she came up with seemed too elaborate and fussy to please Mr. Worthington or too plain and unexciting to please her. Sarah always felt that Christmas was the one time of year when it was such fun to go all out. Surely Mr. Worthington didn't expect her to do nothing more than set up a plate of cold cuts and crackers and play some holiday music over the intercom. No, she'd definitely have to come up with something more festive than that. She needed a cup of coffee while she mulled over all this.

On her way down the hall to the break room, she heard snickers and giggles coming from the secretarial cubicles. Someone whispered, "He gave her a kiss."

Sarah gasped. So Margo had told everyone about the kiss from Mr. Worthington. Well, at least Margo was spreading the truth this time, but it seemed she had left out the most important point. "It was chocolate!" Sarah announced for everyone's benefit.

On her way back from the break room, Sarah made a short detour to Mr. Kent's office. The door was open and he had a putter in his hand. Sarah could see a golf ball on the floor in front of him.

"You busy?"

Mr. Kent looked up. "No, not really. Come in, Sarah. Have a seat." He set down the putter and walked over to the door.

"I hate to bother you," said Sarah.

"No bother. What's up?"

Sarah scrunched up her face. "Well, it's the office Christmas party."

Mr. Kent grinned. "I loved those elves serving flaming snacks last year, and the giant snowman cakes were a hoot, and I still can't figure out how you got it to snow indoors or how you managed that amazing gift exchange." He chuckled just thinking about it all.

Sarah frowned. "But Mr. Worthington doesn't want a party like that this year."

Mr. Kent shook his head in wonder. "I don't know what's with him lately. He's turning into Ebenezer Scrooge. Let me guess. He wants something 'festive, but simple.'"

"Exactly," said Sarah. "And I can't come up with a single idea for a party that is as simple as he seems to want that isn't downright boring. I've looked at magazines, watched the food channel, and I even checked out all sorts of websites and blogs for ideas, but nothing sounds like fun."

After a few seconds, Mr. Kent snapped his fingers. "You know what everyone likes to do during the holidays, don't you?"

Sarah wasn't sure. "Get presents?"

"Well, yeah, but besides that."

Sarah racked her brain. "Eat?"

"Yeah, but what else?"

Sarah felt like a contestant on a game show, a game show she wasn't winning. "I don't know," she said finally.

"Sing Christmas carols and holidays songs, of course," said Mr. Kent.

Now Sarah was confused. "Are you saying we should go carolling for our office party?"

Mr. Kent smirked. "No, no. But it's simple. We should have a karaoke Christmas party."

Sarah tapped her index finger against her lips as she thought about this. "Well...we do have quite a few people here who love to sing."

"And quite a few people who'd love to make Christmas hams of themselves," said Mr. Kent, obviously delighted with his silly pun.

Sarah giggled as she thought about what fun this would be for everyone. "It's perfect," she said. "We can rent a karaoke machine, but what about food...and decorations?"

"No need to rent a machine. We can have the party at a karaoke restaurant...one that has a special room for parties. They may even handle the decorations, and of course they'll take care of the food."

"But Mr. Worthington likes to have the party here at the office," said Sarah. "We always have the Christmas party here."

"Well, this year will be different. You just plan the party by finding the restaurant, Sarah. I'll take care of Charlie Worthington."

Sarah breathed a sigh of relief. "Thank you, Mr. Kent. You've come to my rescue once again. I don't know what I'd do without you."

Mr. Kent moved closer to Sarah and looked into her eyes. "Well, hopefully you'll never have to find out."

Sarah blushed and took a step back. Mr. Kent smelled so good and his eyes were so blue. Feelings began to stir in her that were a bit unsettling. "I need to go now," she said.

Back in her office, Sarah went online to see if there were any karaoke restaurants nearby. The first one she located looked too much like a biker bar from the photos and description on the website. But she finally found a restaurant that seemed a better choice and the website had pictures of nice rooms that were available for private parties. The final hurdle was checking to see if they were open during lunch hours since Mr. Ebenezer Worthington insisted they have the party during the day. Sarah clicked on the menu at the top of the page that said "hours of operation" and was relieved to find they were open for lunch and dinner. She called the restaurant and reserved a private room for December 23rd at noon.

Later that afternoon, Sarah created some party invitations on her computer. She got all the employees' email addresses from Margo and quickly sent out the invitations. When she had finished, she felt proud of herself for keeping things simple.

By the next day, the office was abuzz with talk about the upcoming party.

"Wow! This is the first time we're having the Christmas party away from the office. Way to go, Sarah!" said Margo. "I can't imagine how you were able to pull that off." She winked.

Sarah knew what Margo was thinking. She decided to be blunt with her. "Yes, you can. You think I'm romantically involved with Mr. Worthington so I was able to convince him to do whatever I want. That's not the case, of course. Mr. Worthington just wants to keep the party simple yet festive this year. And having a restaurant handle everything seemed like the best way to do that." Sarah turned and walked away leaving Margo sitting there with her mouth open.

The next morning as Sarah made her way to the break room there were no whispers and no snickers. Sarah was glad she had managed to put the romantic rumors to rest since they weren't true (even though she wished they *were* true). She went back to planning the

Christmas party. She decided to visit the restaurant and meet with the manager.

When she got to the restaurant she asked to see the room they would be using for the party. It was an attractive room, but not very festive. The manager told her that if she wanted it to look "festive" she'd have to bring in her own decorations the night before the party and remove them as soon as the party was over. That wouldn't be a problem. Sarah knew she could get Margo, the decorator, and a few others from the company to help her set up and tear down decorations.

For the next few days, Sarah planned the "simple, yet festive" decorations. And while she wouldn't plan an elaborate gift exchange like last year, she would make sure everyone at the party received a simple gift. When she had her plans all in place she called the decorator. Then she took the company credit card Mr. Worthington had given her and went shopping for all that she needed.

By the time December 23rd rolled around, Sarah had everything ready for the simplest holiday party she had ever planned. She and a few helpers had decorated the room the night before, the menu had been set, and the karaoke machine was all ready with dozens of Christmas songs and carols. She felt confident Mr. Worthington would be pleased. She arrived at the restaurant a bit early, in case any last minute details needed to be taken care of. She had dressed in a simple, fitted Christmassy red dress and black, stiletto-heeled sandals. Her shoulder-length blonde hair was styled in a sleek blunt cut and a pair of silver snowflakes dangled from her earlobes. She had even splurged on a manicure the day before.

Around noon everyone began arriving for the party. Mr. Kent was one of the first. "Wow! You look stunning, Ms. Langley," he said when he saw her.

Sarah blushed. "Why, thank you, Mr. Kent. But what do you think of the room? Is everything simple yet festive enough for Mr. Worthington?"

Mr. Kent looked around at everything. By Worthington's standards the decorations could hardly be called simple—snowflake cut-outs hanging from the ceiling, miniature Christmas trees with twinkling lights on every table, and tiny snowmen place cards with a box of candy at every chair. But by Sarah's standards they were minimal. "It looks very nice," said Mr. Kent.

As more people arrived, Sarah could overhear everyone remarking about how wonderful everything looked.

"Leave it to Sarah to make things special," said Mr. Kent's assistant, Mindy.

"Oh, look! We each get our own box of candy," said Jonathan, who worked in the mailroom.

When the seats were filled, luncheon was served. The menu was simple. Except for dessert. There were no giant snowman cakes, of course, but Sarah had insisted on flaming Christmas puddings — one for each guest. The servers were careful to set them ablaze at different times, however, to keep the smoke detectors from going off.

Mr. Worthington fumed as his Christmas pudding was set on fire. He glared at Sarah. She knew he'd have something to say about this after the party was over. When she'd finally decided on the dessert menu a few days ago, individual Christmas puddings had seemed like such a simple idea…but now, oh, dear. Sarah looked over at Mr. Kent with a desperate look on her face. He immediately came to her rescue by tapping on his water glass with a spoon.

"Attention, everyone. For those of you who have finished dessert, it's time for a little fun and entertainment." Mr. Kent got up from his table and went over to a small stage at the front of the room. "Who would like to start us off with *Rudolph, the Red-nosed Reindeer?*" he asked.

People laughed and many shook their heads. But Margo stood up. Everyone applauded and cheered her on as she took to the stage and grabbed the microphone from Mr. Kent. Her bright red hair contrasted with the green Christmas sweater and black slacks she was wearing. *Leave it to Margo to look festive for a party*, thought Sarah.

Soon Margo had finished the song and a small group in the corner came up to the stage to lead everyone in *Frosty, the Snowman*. Mr. Kent managed to pull Mr. Worthington onto the stage but he couldn't get him to join in on the song. When it ended, Mr. Worthington jumped off the stage and headed out of the room. *Definitely not a good sign*, thought Sarah as Margo came over to her and said, "Great party, as usual, Sarah!"

"Yeah, wonderful party," said Debbie. "This is really fun."

After the party was over, Margo stayed to help Sarah take down the decorations. When they had everything boxed up, they went back to the office to unload the boxes. They had barely walked into the building when

Mr. Worthington appeared. "Ms. Langley, I need to speak to you. Come to my office. Now!"

Sarah gulped then smiled weakly at Margo. "I'll help you unload the boxes if you can wait until I talk with Mr. Worthington."

"Sure," said Margo. Sarah knew Margo would be glad to wait if it meant there would be more juicy gossip to spread round the office after the holidays.

When Sarah got to Mr. Worthington's office he was standing looking out the window. His tie was loosened and he had removed his jacket. Sarah coughed slightly and he turned to face her. "Come in and sit down, Ms. Langley."

Sarah took a seat in the chair across from his desk.

"Ms. Langley, I don't know what your idea of simple, yet festive is, but that crazy karaoke party was the farthest thing from what I asked for. I don't know why I ever let Brad Kent convince me you could plan something simple and have it at a restaurant. Why...you just can't help yourself, can you? You just have to make everything fussy and complicated and over the top!"

Sarah's eyes widened. She felt her pulse race and she realized she was clenching her fists. "I'm so sorry, Mr.

Worthington. I did my best to keep it simple, yet festive. I guess the Christmas puddings were a bit much, but..."

"A bit much? Why, if they'd lit them all at once the fire department would have been called in!"

Sarah felt her bottom lip start to tremble. She didn't know what to say.

"And I certainly did not enjoy being made a fool of, Ms. Langley, by being dragged up on stage to sing some childish song about a snowman with people who work for me!" The vein in Mr. Worthington's temple was starting to bulge and his face had grown bright red. "After the holidays, we will need to rethink your position here as my assistant."

Sarah blinked back the tears. "You mean...you're going to fire me?"

Mr. Worthington sat down at his desk and looked at Sarah. "I don't know, Ms. Langley. I honestly don't know. But that is all right now. You may go."

Sarah stood up. "Merry...Merry Christmas, Mr. Worthington" she managed to say before she rushed out of the room. She passed Margo in the hall on the way to her office. She slammed the door and sat at her desk sobbing uncontrollably. A few minutes later she heard someone tapping on the door.

"Sarah? Are you okay?" It was Mr. Kent. "Can I come in?" He eased open the door before Sarah could answer. "Oh, Sarah, what happened? What's wrong?"

Sarah grabbed a tissue from her desk and wiped her eyes. She didn't want Mr. Kent to see her blubbering like this. She sniffled and tried to talk. "It's Mr. Worthington. He hated the party!"

"He what? How could he? It was a wonderful party!" said Mr. Kent.

Sarah sniffled again. "He said it was the farthest thing from what he wanted. And...and he said that after the holidays he's going to rethink my position here as his assistant. Oh, Mr. Kent, I think he's going to fire me!" Suddenly, Sarah was sobbing again.

Mr. Kent sat down in the chair beside her and took her hands. "Look at me, Sarah," he said. "I probably shouldn't say this, but Charlie Worthington is a fool. He doesn't appreciate how wonderful you are! I hope he does fire you."

Sarah pulled away from him. "What? How can you say that?"

"I say that for two reasons, Sarah."

"Two reasons? I don't understand, Mr. Kent," said Sarah, wiping her eyes again.

"Well, first you shouldn't be working for a man who doesn't appreciate you. In fact, you shouldn't be working for anyone at all. You should start your own company."

Sarah couldn't believe what she was hearing. "My own company?"

"Yes, your own event-planning company. You'd be wonderful! You *are* wonderful, Sarah! People love your parties. They love the way you make things so special."

Sarah started to smile, remembering all the compliments she had gotten earlier at the party. "They do, don't they?"

"Yes, they do," said Mr. Kent.

"But my own company…I don't have the money to start my own company even if I knew what to do to start a company, which I don't."

"I'll help you get a loan," said Mr. Kent. "Better yet. I'll loan you the money to get started. And I'll help you figure out what to do."

Sarah gulped. Mr. Kent must really believe in her if he was willing to loan her his own money. Mr. Worthington had *never* believed in her like that. She began to wonder why she ever thought Mr. Worthington was the man for her. But then she remembered something. "You said there were two reasons you hope Mr. Worthington will fire me. What's the other reason?"

Mr. Kent looked into her teary eyes. "Oh, Sarah, can't you guess? Isn't it obvious that I've been in love with you since I first saw you?"

Sarah felt her heart flutter. "What? But you never said anything."

"I couldn't," said Mr. Kent, "Not with Charlie's silly rule about no dating within the company. But don't you see? If he fires you, that means we're free to see each other."

Sarah could hardly believe what she was hearing. How could she have been so blind? How could she have ever thought of Mr. Kent as a helpful big brother — so that was why he looked so strange that day she told him she felt that way.

Sarah made up her mind then and there. She was finished trying to please Mr. Worthington. She was finished trying to adhere to the stupid K. I. S. S. principle. "Mr. Worthington won't have to fire me," she said. "I quit." She reached over and took the huge Hershey's Kiss® and threw it in the trash. She opened the door and Margo almost fell into the room.

"You need to see this, Margo," said Sarah, "so you get the facts exactly right."

Sarah reached for Brad Kent and wrapped her arms around his neck. Then she gave him a long, sweet Christmas kiss. And it was definitely *not* chocolate!

THE ESCAPE ARTIST

Wendy Dewar Hughes

Just a little bit more. If Laura could stretch just a little bit farther, she wouldn't have to get down off the ladder and move the thing. One more flick of the brush on the inside of this window would do it, she thought, leaning far out over the top of the stepladder, and then she could go home.

At the same moment Laura twisted her wrist to put the final curlicue on the end of a sprig of holly, a figure appeared in the window. That's all it took to make her lose her concentration . . . and her balance. The ladder teetered and tilted. The jar of paint slid off the ladder's shelf and crashed to the floor spraying Christmas green in a goopy fan on the store's pale floor tiles. Laura's arms

173

windmilled backwards but it didn't help. She was going over and in about a half second would land face first in a bulk bin of dog food.

Suddenly, the door flew open and a figure leapt through it, lunging into the line of Laura's descent. He threw his arms open wide, catching her in mid-air but the paint on the floor was his undoing. As her weight hit his body, his feet slipped out from beneath him and the two of them crashed to the floor in the pool of sticky, green paint. The ladder clattered to the floor beside them.

"Umph!" Laura grunted when she had stopped flying. She lay on top of the stranger who stared up at her with the brownest eyes she had ever seen. His thick brown hair had already begun soaking up green paint.

"Ouch," he said, blinking. "I think I've broken my head."

Laura tried to push away from him but started to laugh. Her hand slipped in the paint and she rolled away, ending up on her back in the paint puddle, her long chestnut hair sticking in the paint.

"Are you sure?" she said, looking sideways at him. "It doesn't look broken to me. It is beginning to look a little green, though."

"I didn't expect you to be so heavy," the man said, pushing up to a sitting position. "Oh, wait. Wrong thing to say. What I meant was, gosh, I'm getting weak. I have *got* to eat more protein."

"I was thinking the same thing," she said scrambling to her feet and gingerly stepping out of the paint puddle. Her shoes left green tracks on the pale grey tiles. She stretched out a hand to help him up. "Laura Dunsmore. Thanks for breaking my fall."

The man gripped her paint-slicked hand and leapt to his feet. "Pleased to meet you. Gareth McTavish, the gallant, obviously."

"Gallant and green, I'd say," Laura observed. "You're a mess."

Gareth bent in an extravagant bow, sweeping his fingertips through the paint at his feet and dragging them across his cheeks. "There! A gentleman and a highlander," he said. "Why don't you let me clean this mess up?"

Store manager Fred Morgan walked up the aisle between the rows of bale twine and the sacks of water softener salt. "What on earth happened here?" he said, scowling at the mess of paint splashed across the front of the store.

"Sorry, Fred," Laura said. "I fell off the ladder and this man charged through the door just in time to keep me from nose-diving into the dog food. If you'll point me toward a mop and bucket, I'll get it cleaned up before you're ready to close."

Without a word, Fred twisted his torso and pointed a meaty finger toward the back of the store. "You might as well help too, Gareth. I won't say that stunts like this happen every day but often enough. If you're going to manage this place you might as well jump in at the deep end."

Laura glanced from Fred to Gareth and back again. "You two know each other?"

"Sure," Fred replied. "Gareth is my wife's sister's son, fresh out of college with a business degree and wanting to get into the farm supply business. I've just taken him on as assistant manager. I want to go south this winter."

Forty-five minutes later, there was hardly a trace of green paint anywhere except in the crevices between the floor tiles. Laura promised to attack those thin green lines the next day.

"Naw," Fred told her, "Gareth can do it. I'm sure you've got plenty to do already. It won't hurt him to do a little grunt work. You done the window?"

"It was that last lick of paint on this one that sent me flying. I didn't want to climb down and move the ladder."

Fred chuckled. "Go on. Come back tomorrow for the other side. I know you have choir practice tonight, anyway."

The lights from the sanctuary spilled pools of golden brightness onto the snow that had drifted in elegant curves around the front of the church. Someone had come by during the day and shovelled the walk, sprinkling salt and sand on the concrete. Laura pulled open the big wooden door and stepped inside, squinting against the sudden brightness.

Carl Adamson spotted her and called to the others milling around the front of the church. "We can start now. Our soprano is here."

Laura stamped the snow from her boots then slipped out of them and set them on a nearby rug. Jogging up the aisle in her socks, she plopped down on the front pew and pulled on a pair of flats to keep her feet warm during practice. The other singers, all fourteen of them, lined up on the low stage as their director, Marion Seifert, took her place at the piano.

"Okay, gang," she called out. "We're only waiting for one more person to show up. We have a new member, a baritone. We'll have to bring him up to speed on the new songs tonight."

As though on cue, the church door swung open and a tall man stepped in. Standing in the dim foyer, Laura didn't recognize him but when he began walking up the aisle, she saw that it was none other than Gareth McTavish.

"Did you get the green out?" she asked as he walked past her.

Gareth skidded to a stop and looked down at Laura. "Check it out," he said, leaning his head toward her.

Laura glanced up a Gareth and noted a green tinge still on the tips of his hair. She grinned and shrugged one shoulder. "Time to sing, highlander," she said, hopping to her feet and joining the choir. Marion situated Gareth right behind Laura and when they began to sing *Go Tell it on the Mountain*, she heard his rich baritone voice soar.

After the practice, Laura gathered up her coat and purse and headed for the door. Before she could get her boots on, Gareth stepped up beside her.

"Highlander to flying artist," he said. "How about grabbing a coffee with me? The Hot Bean is open until ten tonight."

"No thanks," Laura said. "Maybe some other time." *Or maybe not,* she thought as she yanked on her boot and walked out, leaving Gareth staring after her.

CHAPTER TWO

Fred Morgan didn't believe in decorating for Christmas before December first. In fact, even the idea of decorating a farm supply store made him itchy but he loved Christmas and his wife Delia wouldn't let him get away with doing nothing.

Laura showed up as soon as the store opened to finish the artwork in the second window. If she could finish this job before noon that would leave her the entire afternoon to work on packing up her paintings to ship to her list of galleries. It was tough work and every time she had to get out the crates and hammer, she promised herself that next time she would get help. She was an artist, after all, not a carpenter.

About the time Laura dabbed the last splotches of paint on the inside of the window — careful not to lean too far this time — Gareth walked through the front door.

"Well, hello," he said, looking up at her. "Would you like me to hold the ladder, or just catch you when you leap off again?"

"My flying career is over," Laura said, stepping down and wiping her brush on a rag. "I'm all done here." She twisted the lid on the paint container and set it in her carryall.

"About last night..."

"You have a great voice," Laura interrupted. "I'm glad you've joined the choir."

"That's not what I meant," he said.

"I have to go," she said, cutting him off again. "I've got a lot of work to do. Would you mind returning the ladder to the back room for me?" He nodded, bewildered, and watched as Laura threw on her jacket, grabbed her bag, and ran out the door.

When Laura came through the front door of the suite she rented in a lovely house in the oldest neighbourhood in town, her cat, Purdy, bounced off the sofa and sauntered over to curl her fluffy body around Laura's leg.

"Hello to you, too," she said, scratching the cat's neck. Setting her gear down by the door, she pulled her boots off, flung her coat on the rack, and headed for the kitchen. "I will not get involved," she muttered to herself. "So the best way to do that is not to give him the time of day." *But he's so cute*, her mind argued. "Derek was cute, too," she countered out loud, "and look what happened there."

Reaching into the fridge for leftover coleslaw and a piece of fried chicken, she couldn't help reviewing yet again the events of exactly three months before. Her wedding dress, freshly steamed and ready for her to wear down the aisle, hung in the closet. Flowers were to be delivered in a couple of hours. That's when her doorbell rang. It was Derek. Her mind went over every word, how he had told her it had all been a big mistake; he couldn't get married, not to her or maybe anyone. *At least*, she thought, *he didn't leave me for another woman. That would have been like a knife to the gut.* No, he left her the morning of the wedding, for a mountain!

She reached for a tissue and soaked up fresh tears, for about the four thousandth time over the past several weeks. There was some stupid mountain in South America that he just had to climb and since she didn't want to climb it with him—good grief!—he thought it best if they called off the wedding.

Since then, Laura had put the wedding gown into a zippered plastic bag and hung it in the back of her closet. She didn't want to see it or even think about it. The relatives had gone home, taking their gifts with them. The food for the reception was distributed amongst the family and friends or given to the local shelter. No, the thought of getting involved with a man again practically made her nauseated.

She clicked on the television to put all thoughts of men and love out of her mind. But from somewhere in the depths of her awareness those brown eyes kept smiling at her.

By nine o'clock, Laura had only three paintings left to crate but decided to call it a night and set the hammer down. Laura was able to keep a studio at home, working in the converted garage that her landlady had included in her rent. The following day she had only one store window to paint, a small one. Since window painting was merely a seasonal sideline for her, she accepted only a few clients.

Even though her energy had almost run out, she couldn't resist picking up a paintbrush and patting a few strokes of colour on her work in progress; but before the paint touched the canvas the doorbell rang.

Who can that be at this hour? she wondered, setting the brush down on her palette. The moment she reached for the doorknob she no longer had to guess. Gareth McTavish stood outside, smiling at her through the square window in the door. She flipped the deadbolt and opened the door.

"Think of me as Mohammed," he said, grinning. In one hand he held a cardboard cup holder containing two paper coffee cups; in the other, a tiny bouquet of flowers.

"Who? Why?"

"Mohammed," he replied. "You know, if the mountain won't come to Mohammed then..."

"...Mohammed will come to the mountain," she finished. "And here I thought you were a highlander, or Sir Galahad, or something. Well, don't stand out there freezing. You might as well come in." She stood aside and allowed him to enter. "What are you doing here? Don't you realize what time it is? And who told you where I live?"

"Boy, you ask a lot of questions," he said, handing her the flowers. "I bought two decaf lattes. They're both the same so you can take your pick."

She sighed and took one of the cups then went to the tiny adjoining kitchen and plopped the flowers into a mug she filled with water. "You haven't answered my questions yet."

"Right. Bringing you flowers and coffee; yes, I do realize what time it is," he ticked the items off on his fingers. "And, Fred."

Laura frowned at him. "Fred what?"

"Gave me your address."

"You're kidding! I'm going to have a word with him," she muttered. "Okay, you've done what you came for, so I think you should go now."

"Oh." Clearly, this wasn't the reception Gareth had been hoping for and Laura felt almost mean for not inviting him to stay for a while. But she had to be firm with herself.

"Sorry if I'm not very friendly tonight but it's late and I have work tomorrow."

"I see," he replied. "In that case, I won't torment you further with goodies and flowers. Ta ta for now." In the next second he was gone.

Laura took one sip of the latte and poured the rest down the sink. It tasted bitter to her now.

CHAPTER THREE

On Saturday morning, Laura sat at her desk going over invoices, bank statements and bills. She ran a hand through her hair, tapping the calculator again. Yes, they added up, she thought, but no, her earning wouldn't cover it all. She needed another source of income this month. When her cell phone rang next to her, she jumped.

"Hi, Dad," she answered after reading the display.

"Hi, kiddo. You busy?"

"Just going over some paperwork. What's up?"

"I could really use an extra pair of hands. I got a big contract to replace all the locks, inside and out, over at that big plastics factory south of town. I'd do it myself but they want the entire job done by next weekend and they have over fifty doors. Can you help me out?"

This is an answer to prayer, she thought, and she hadn't even prayed yet. The window painting gigs had all been done and all her artwork shipped but she wouldn't be paid until sometime in January.

"Sure I can," she answered. "Just tell me when and where and I'll be there with my own tools. Actually, I'll come by the house in a little while and get you to take a look at them. I haven't used these tools for quite a while." Laura's father, the town's leading locksmith, had taught her the craft when she was a young teen and though she had yet to choose it as a profession, the knowledge sometimes came in handy.

Later that afternoon, Laura glanced at the clock and realized that if she wanted to get to the drugstore to pick up more shampoo and toothpaste, she had to hurry, as stores would soon close. Grabbing her jacket, she slipped on her warm boots and gloves, stuffed the folder of locksmithing tools in her purse and headed out. She knew it took a good fifteen minutes to walk from her suite to downtown and since she had been sedentary all day, working on her bookkeeping, the walk would do her good. She set off in high spirits with her face to the winter sunshine.

After picking up what she needed at the drugstore she wandered toward her dad's house, gazing in the store windows at their Christmas displays. With only a few weeks until Christmas, she could sense excitement building. Young mothers went by, trailing children or pushing strollers on the salted sidewalks. The flower shop window overflowed with poinsettias and evergreen wreaths. A ladies' fashion store flaunted sparkling cocktail dresses and shimmering sweaters.

When she came to the feed store at the far end of the block, she stopped to give her artistic handiwork an objective appraisal. Holly and evergreen boughs trailed through the swooping letters of *Merry Christmas* and *Season's Greetings.* This year she had created a new design for Fred and she liked it.

Suddenly, a face appeared in the circle of the O in Season's. Brown eyes smiled out at her and in a moment, Gareth pulled open the door.

"Come in," he said, motioning her forward.

"No, I'm on my way to my dad's house."

"Oh, come on. I promise not to try anything gallant. I need your help." He reached for her hand and pulled her into the store. Then he whipped a ring of keys from his belt and locked the door.

"What are you doing?" Laura asked, eyeing him with suspicion.

He gave her a quizzical look. "It's time to close. I was just about to do that when I saw you out there."

"So, what do you want from me?"

Gareth led her to the back of the store and reached under the cash counter. "I've been going over the music for the choir and I can't get this part right. It's hard to practice when you don't have a piano. If you can sing your part, maybe I can find my notes."

Laura sighed. "All right, let me see the music."

Gareth pointed out the bar where he claimed to be having trouble and Laura found the soprano line. Her voice lifted on the notes and his came in perfectly. They went over it a couple of times then she said, "You're not having trouble with this section at all. You've nailed it every time." She crossed her arms and looked at him.

"That's only because you're here singing the right notes," he said, smiling.

"Well, now that you've got it, I'll get going." She picked her purse up from the counter and walked to the door, waiting for him to unlock it.

When he stood beside her, he tilted his head. "Oh look," he said, "it's locked. I guess you're stuck in here with me."

Laura remembered the tools in her purse. Pulling the folder out, she selected a pick, fiddled with the lock for a few seconds then pulled the door open. Slipping through it she said, "See you later, highlander."

As she walked past the window she glanced back to see Gareth standing there shaking his head.

Choir practices had been stepped up from once a week to three times a week as the special Carol Service night at the church approached. Laura spent her days working with her father at the factory lock job and alternate evenings painting as though a fire had lit her soul. She didn't understand it but a renewed creativity had seized her and she found herself almost in a frenzy of painting, sometimes long into the night.

One the other nights of the week, the choir practices went overtime. They had eleven Christmas carols to perform and everyone dove into the practice with zeal. While singing, Laura tried to concentrate on the music and the leader but she found herself acutely aware that Gareth stood just behind her. She could hear his rich baritone voice flowing over her and enveloping her in its lustrous sounds. She could even smell his aftershave with each intake of breath. By the end of each practice she felt almost intoxicated with his nearness.

"What's the matter with you today?" Laura's dad asked her one day as she fiddled with a new lock that she couldn't seem to get in place properly. "Where is your head?"

Laura looked up at him from her kneeling position. "What do you mean?"

"You've done the same thing three times and you still haven't got it right. Do you want me to take over on this one?"

"No, Dad. I'm getting it. I guess I'm just a little tired. We've been practising a lot for the Carol Service."

"Mm-hmm," he responded with a nod. "I hear Fred Morgan has a new assistant manager working for him. Says he's a pretty good singer."

Laura flinched involuntarily and dropped her screwdriver. Letting go of the doorknob in her hands, she sat back on her heels. "What's that got to do with anything?" she asked.

"Maybe nothing. Maybe something. Fred tells me this guy — Garth, is it? He's pretty interested in you."

"It's Gareth," she replied, a little too fast. She looked up at her father. "You know I don't want to get involved with anyone. After what Derek did, I don't think I could stand to have that happen again."

"Honey, one bad apple doesn't spoil the whole bunch. Maybe you should give this guy a chance. Fred tells me he's a super guy, real quality."

Laura's head swam with visions of Gareth's gorgeous brown eyes and the remembered scent of his cologne. "I just can't," was all she said. Then she picked up the screwdriver and attacked the doorknob again.

CHAPTER FOUR

With only four days to go until the big performance, Laura found herself getting more and more keyed up. What annoyed her more than the butterflies doing gymnastic manoeuvres in her stomach was the fact that she didn't know why she felt so stressed. She loved singing in the choir and had never been nervous. In the past, she had even sung solo parts without so much as a flutter, so being a bag of ragged nerves unsettled her even more.

After the practice, she set her music down and was about to follow the others toward the door when a hand caught her arm. "Hey, Laura, I need to talk to you. I know you're not much for coffee at this time of night but neither of us can get away from work during the day. Can I walk you home?"

Laura hesitated for a moment then sighed. "Sure, you can walk me home."

Once outside in the clear night air, Laura looked up at the stars scattered across the indigo sky like handfuls of flung glitter. She felt Gareth take her elbow and ease her down the church steps. "What's on your mind?" she asked when they reached the bottom and started down the walk.

"I have to make a decision about my job," he said, "and I don't have many friends in town I can talk to. In fact, you're about the only one."

She flashed him a sideways glance but said nothing.

"I can't really talk to anyone from the choir and I can't talk to Fred either since it involves him."

"What about your family?" Laura ventured. "Your folks?"

"My dad passed away last year and my mom is still kind of having a hard time with that. I don't want to burden her and my one sister just gave birth to twins so I think she's a little pre-occupied."

"Okay, well, since you've narrowed confidants down to me, what is it?"

"I got a job offer. I love working with Fred — don't get me wrong. And I know if I stay here, one day he'll probably offer to sell me the business since he has no kids of his own. It's just that this other job pays a lot more and might be a step up to something bigger. I'm just not sure if I should take it."

"Where is it?" Laura asked.

"Well, that's the other problem. It's about seven hundred miles from here in a town called Watsonville. The store is a chain so I could work my way up to company management if I wanted. They say there's plenty of room for upward mobility."

"Why is that a problem?" Laura asked, brushing snowflakes from her coat. "If it's what you want to do, what would stop you?"

"Well, that's just it. It's not the only thing I want." He stopped walking and threw his head back. "You see that star up there?" he said, pointing. "That really bright one?"

Laura looked up. With the sky as full of stars as grains of sand on the seashore, she wasn't at all sure which one he meant but played along. "Yes."

"It reminds me of you. It's like I've been surrounded by plain, ordinary, look-alike stars all my life, and then suddenly, one shines brighter than all the rest."

Laura levelled her gaze on him. When he turned to look into her eyes, she could even see his warm brown ones in the light from the streetlamp. "Whoa," she said. "Are you trying to tell me that you're thinking of not taking that job because of me?" She took a step backwards.

"Laura, you're the kind of woman that I've been waiting — no, searching, for. When I met you I thought, that's it. I've arrived at the destination. I can't stop thinking about you. I know you've been avoiding me and

I think I understand why but it's like you're an escape artist, always slipping through my fingers."

"You don't understand," she said, choking out the words. "I don't know if Fred told you this but three months ago I was ready to march up the aisle of that church back there to get married." She dropped her head and swallowed hard. "He abandoned me the morning of the wedding."

"I know and I'm so sorry. If you need more time or more room, I can give you that but it's you I want. I know that."

Panic churned up from Laura's gut into her chest, grabbing her by the throat. *This can't be happening*, she thought, casting about for something to hang onto. Gareth's arm was the only thing within reach but she dared not touch it.

"Oh no," she said, backing up another step. "No, you've got it all wrong. I'm not the one for you. I'm not the one for anyone." With that she turned and ran, ran without stopping or looking back until she reached her apartment. Jamming her key in the lock, she flung open the door then slammed it behind her and locked it. Without turning on a light, she hurled herself onto the sofa as great, wrenching sobs were torn from her body.

"What on earth happened to you?" Laura's dad asked her the next morning when she showed up for work. "You look like you've either been sick all night or carousing all night. Which is it?"

"Neither. There's nothing wrong with me," Laura protested, reaching in her bag for her tools.

"Honey, you can fool some of the people," her dad said, reaching out to take her by the arms, "but I'm your old dad and you can't fool me. What is it? You haven't been yourself for days and now you look like tram smash-up." He ducked to be in the line of her lowered gaze, forcing her to look at him.

"It's Gareth," she said as a single tear slid down the side of her cheek. "Last night he told me that he's been offered a job but he's thinking of not taking it because he thinks I'm the woman of his dreams, or something."

"I have no trouble believing that you're all that to someone," he said. "I'm guessing, however, that the feeling isn't mutual. Am I right?"

Laura nodded. "After Derek, I decided to have nothing to do with anyone else. I don't want to put myself in that position ever again. It hurt too much."

Her dad folded her into his arms and rocked her to and fro, kissing the top of her head. "Honey, you can't build a wall around your heart. Loving means that you set yourself up for hurt. I loved your mom for thirty-five years. Don't you think it hurt like crazy when she died?"

"Of course," Laura agreed into his shoulder. "But that's different."

"No, it's not. You loved Derek and he left but that doesn't mean Gareth is going to do the same thing. There are no guarantees in life but if you never love or allow yourself to be loved you'll miss out on the best life has to offer."

Laura pulled away and sniffed loudly. Her father drew a soft, cotton handkerchief from his pocket and handed it to her. "You may not be ready to try again just yet but don't make it a forever decision."

"Okay. I just know I'm not ready for anything right now."

"Then you owe it to Gareth to tell him."

CHAPTER FIVE

The Carol Service had been scheduled for December 15th, a Sunday evening. By mid-afternoon it had begun to snow, first lazy flakes that spiralled down from a dove-coloured sky; then as darkness fell the snowfall become a cascade of fluffy spheres that floated to the ground and glowed in the lights from the streetlamps. It muffled the sound of traffic and voices and lent a magical aura to the evening.

Laura arrived early as required, gathering with the other choir members in the church basement to dress in their dark blue gowns. She couldn't help but notice how the colour of the fabric accentuated the rich brown of Gareth's eyes but every time his met hers, she looked away. They had hardly spoken since the night she had run away from him, except at the dress rehearsal. As she was pulling on her boots the previous night, he crouched on the floor beside her.

"I've accepted the position," he said softly. She straightened up and looked down into his upturned face, a face filled with sorrow and longing.

"That's probably the right decision," she replied. "I wish you all the best."

"If you say the word, I'll stay."

"Gareth, I can't do that. I'm not ready for any kind of commitment and it wouldn't be fair of me to suggest that I ever will be."

"Okay," he said. He stood to his feet and, pulling on his coat, went out the door without a backward glance.

The Carol Service was beautiful, peaceful and blessed. At least that's what everyone said. Laura went through the motions and remembered all the words to the songs. But it was like someone else sang, looked out at the audience and took the bows. As soon as the performance was over, she hurried to the basement, hung up her choir gown, and left by the back door. She never saw Gareth watch her go.

The days counted down until Christmas and Laura used the time to paint a whole new series of canvases for the galleries that represented her. As though the artist had been seized with an almost feverish intensity, the new work took on a quality dissimilar from anything she had done previously. The colours glowed with depth and vibrancy; the shapes seemed to almost lift off the canvases. She threw all her energy into these canvases, often working long into the night. The job with her father had ended five days prior to Christmas so she didn't have to get up early for work. Instead, she painted until late and slept in late. When she wasn't painting or sleeping, she went for long walks in the park, forging her own paths through the sometimes knee-deep snow, relishing the silence and thinking about Gareth. After the big snowfall, the weather had turned sunny and clear and the snow sparkled like fields of crystals. Laura hardly noticed.

Laura and her father had decided to have a quiet Christmas day then go away for a few days between Christmas and New Year's. "A little change of scenery," he explained. "It'll do us good."

She knew he was trying to make her feel better so she smiled, kissed his cheek and agreed. On Christmas Eve, Laura packed a sack full of gifts that she had bought for her father. He always insisted that he neither wanted nor needed anything but she had found a few things she knew he would enjoy — tickets to the symphony in January, a GPS for his pickup truck, and a big box of his favourite cream-filled chocolates. She fed the cat and was about to pull on her coat and boots when she heard scuffling outside the door, followed by a light knocking.

Switching on the outdoor light, she peered through the glass. Gareth gazed back at her.

"I thought you'd gone," she said when she opened the door.

"I did," he said. "I came back."

"Then you'd better come in."

He stamped the snow off his boots and stepped into the room, dripping on the rug by the door.

"I was about to go see my dad," Laura began but stopped when he lifted a hand.

"This won't take long," Gareth said. "Do you mind if I sit down for a minute?"

"Of course not." She indicated a spot on the sofa, moved the cat off a chair and sat down opposite him.

"I brought you a present," he said as though suddenly remembering, and reached into his capacious coat pocket. He handed her a wrapped cylinder about the size of a can of tomatoes. "Open it."

She tore off the paper and smiled. Inside was a jar of green paint.

"I figured you could use it since your other jar ended up on my backside."

"Thanks," she said simply. "Now tell me why you're really here."

"I couldn't do it," he said. "I took the job and they wanted me to start right away. Fred was kind enough to let me go without giving notice once I explained what a big opportunity it was. He's a good guy, Fred."

"I know."

"Anyway, when the manager at the other company started showing me around their operation, I just began getting this sick feeling in my stomach, like I'd eaten some bad clams or too many Brussels sprouts. With every step I took, I felt worse. Then I couldn't even concentrate on what he was saying. His voice sounded like a terrible cell phone connection. By the time we got back to his office to sign papers, I had to tell him that I had changed my mind. All I could think about was you, here, working in your studio, painting windows, flying off ladders. I wanted to be here, to be the one to catch you." He stopped talking then and looked at the gloves he'd been twisting in his hands. "Well, that's about it. Fred gave me my job back. He told me he figured I might not stay over there. I just wanted you to know that I came back for you. If you don't want me, well, I'll just have to live with that but I couldn't go through the rest of my life wishing that I had told you I love you. I wanted you to know that."

He stood to go and turned toward the door.

"Wait!" Laura said, springing up from her chair. He spun back toward her. "I'm so sorry," she whispered." Since you've been gone, I haven't been able to think about anything else but you. All I've done is paint and sleep and think of you."

"So..."

"I don't know where this can go or if I'm ready for anything but I'm glad you came back." She took a step toward him. "Christmas without you was looking a little bleak."

"Does that mean you like me?"

Laura nodded. "Yes, I like you. I like you a lot."

"And sometimes you'll even go for coffee with me?"

"Sure," she said, biting her lip.

"No more escape artist moves then?"

She shook her head. "No more, I promise."

"No more flying off ladders?"

"I can't guarantee that but I'll try to remember to get down and move the ladder next time."

"Good," he said, his eyes bright, "because I really do think I broke my head with that fall. And you very nearly broke my heart."

"Well," she said, reaching for his hand, "if I ever need someone to break my fall again, I want it to be you."

TAKE A CHANCE ON US

Barbara Glover

I was homeless, living at the mission. The mission fed the hungry and poverty-stricken and contained five housing units where people could stay for a month or so to get on their feet. My three-year-old daughter, Zoe, and I were staying in one of these units, and I helped out during mealtimes. There were free laundry machines in the basement and apartments on the two levels above the kitchen rented at Provincial Housing rates. I was hoping to get a job and move into one of those apartments soon.

He was a regular at the mission, helping to feed the homeless and less fortunate. Everyone knew and liked him for his easy manner and jokes. I loved his blue eyes and the unruly mop of chestnut brown curls and his almost shaven, but not quite, look. He was rugged, and muscles rippled when he moved. I knew he played the guitar because he serenaded the clients during meals from time to time. His name was Sheldon.

"Would you like to grab a coffee once we've cleaned up here?" he asked one day. It was obvious he didn't think I was one of the homeless. He thought I was a volunteer.

I was caught off guard. He joked with the people in line but rarely spoke to anyone else. "Sorry. Other commitments. How about a rain check?" I said.

"Sure. Thursday?" he asked.

I smiled. "Sorry, laundry day."

"Come on, take a chance on us."

"Sorry. I really do have laundry."

"Are you washing your hair, too?"

"What? No. Oh, I see. No. I have a three-year-old. She's going to need clean clothes pretty soon, so I've cleared my calendar to do laundry on Thursday. Not exciting but it has to be done."

"Need help?"

I was surprised. "Uh, sure, I guess. I do laundry in the basement here. It's convenient," I added, thinking that would keep him from figuring out where we were living.

He seemed fine with that explanation. "Just so you know, my mother fully believed in child labour," he said. "My brothers and I were doing laundry at age eleven. I'm still pretty good at throwing a fabric softener sheet in the dryer." He smiled showing even white teeth.

"Okay. Thursday, 1:30, mission laundry room. You're in charge of the fabric softener sheets," I said.

"I'm looking forward to it." He put on his coat and left.

*Looking forward to it…*his words made my heart beat a little faster. No one had paid any attention to me since my divorce—no one except Zoe, and she was a little selfish when it came to attention.

Thursday I was in the laundry room by 1:00 so he wouldn't see us leaving our unit. I was busy sorting laundry when I heard Zoe giggle. I turned to see him kneeling before her with a stuffed elephant.

"You are almost as pretty as your mom. Did you know that, Princess?" he asked.

She held out her arms to be picked up. He lifted her high in the air, and she squealed in delight as he carried her over to me.

"Tea, black," he said, depositing Zoe on the dryer beside me and handing me a plastic cup. "Cream and sugar on the side." He pulled a packet of sugar and a little container of creamer from his pocket and set them beside the cup.

We got to know each other through light banter and a game he called 'Five Questions, Two Passes'. "I'll ask five questions and you can pass on any two of them, the rest you have to answer."

I nodded. Sounded like fun.

"Where were you raised?" he asked.

"Hoddeston, Herts, England."

"That explains the accent. Why did you move?"

"I married. Husband got a job here."

"Where is said husband?" he asked.

"Pass."

"Hobbies?"

"Yes." I grinned.

"That wasn't a real answer. You have to do better than that," he said.

"Okay, horseback riding, lawn bowling…"

"Lawn bowling? Who lawn bowls these days? Are you any good at it?"

"That was seven questions and isn't fair according to your rules," I said.

He smiled. "You caught me off guard with the lawn bowling. Makes me think of old people with canes and white hair, not someone so young and beautiful as you. Is there a group in the city?"

"Sorry, question period is up."

The afternoon was fun. He sorted and folded clothes and played with Zoe. I found myself telling him of my failed marriage and lack of a job. I did not tell him I was homeless. I couldn't bear that. It was nice having someone take an interest in Zoe and me.

"Dinner later?" he asked.

"I need to put the clothes away and the princess needs to be in bed by 7:00 or she turns into a dragon."

"Okay. I have an hour of work to do. Why don't I pick you up at 4:30 and we can go to the little diner down the street? I'll have you home by 6:00. Bath, jammies, story, and bed by 7:00. What do you think?"

I think that was when he took a piece of my heart.

"Thanks, we'd love that. How about we meet you at the diner at 4:30? We don't live very far."

"Sure thing. Need help getting this stuff home?"

"No, we'll be fine."

"See you later then." He knelt down and gave Zoe a hug. "Be good for Mom, Princess." Her response was to try and stick the elephant's trunk up his nose.

Later that evening, we ate, laughed, shared stories, then played in the snow in the park a block away, running amid the gaily lit pine trees. The falling snow only added to the magical feeling and made me think we were the only people in the world. We were running and playing tag with Zoe when suddenly I was showered in snow as he shook a branch. I chased him, and as I caught him, he turned and grabbed me and we both tumbled into the snow. The world stood still. He and I were the only two people on the planet. Everything disappeared into nothingness. This was where I belonged. I felt I had come home. He reached up and cupped my cheek in his hand then raised his head. Stars exploded in my brain and I thought for sure there were fireworks. I didn't know it then, but that was when I gave him my heart...all of it. Only Zoe trying to poke her small head between us brought me back to reality.

When it was time to go, I was adamant we didn't need anyone to walk us home, but he came as far as the mission, then he went in one direction and Zoe and I in the other before we backtracked to our unit there.

Later, lying beside Zoe enveloped in the dark, I replayed the day in my mind. It had been so long since anyone cared about me. Yet, I still found it hard to believe that Zoe and I were living in a mission unit these days because my now ex-husband, Ted, decided he needed new eye-candy hanging from his arm, and Zoe and I were flung aside like rag dolls with no warning or preparation. I had no job and no skills, having married right out of high school, then moving to a different country, and having a baby a year later. I was seeking maintenance for Zoe, and the courts did move, but sometimes very slowly. It was all demeaning and embarrassing. The life I was living now was so far from everything I had known, and no one from my previous life would even dream I was here. I had often thought of returning home, but I couldn't take Zoe out of the country. I was stuck. This Christmas, which was fast approaching, was going to be different and difficult.

On Tuesday, Sheldon came in late and surprised me by saying, "There is a job opening at The Health Centre. They need a receptionist from 8:00 to 4:00 to answer phones, do some typing, take care of the mail, greet the patients, and such. The daycare will have a spot open for

Zoe if you need a sitter. You should take a resume down. The posting closes Friday at noon."

It sounded good, so I decided to give it a shot, and I was lucky enough to get an interview a few days later. After the job interview Shelly, the interviewer, took me around the building. She showed me the daycare and I met the staff. Through one office window, I saw Sheldon dressed in a suit leaning over a desk.

"I thought he worked at the hospital?" I said, surprised.

"Mr. Lamb? He's our director. His offices are at the hospital, but he comes by at least twice a week to oversee things. He's worked extremely hard at getting the mental health piece in place here, which is why we'll need a fulltime receptionist. With three more employees on board it will be very busy around here."

"Director? I had assumed he worked in laundry or housekeeping, or was an aide," I replied.

"No, not at all. In fact, he handpicks many of the people he wants to work here. That's part of the reason he volunteers at the mission. Many people here have jobs because of him."

So I was his charity case. He must have seen where we went that night after we finished the laundry and felt sorry for us. I fumed all the way back to the mission. I couldn't turn down the job if Zoe and I were to become independent, but I would not stand for *his* charity.

"Things are a little frosty in here even though the soup is hot," commented Sheldon Thursday at lunch.

I kept working and ignored him.

"Is something wrong? Have I offended you somehow?" he asked.

"I'm not your charity case. You lied to me."

"I never said you were. What are you talking about?" he asked.

"The job. I got the job as receptionist, and I am grateful because now I can provide for Zoe, but you had it all planned out beforehand. It was no accident I got that job, was it? I didn't get it because of any skills I have. I don't want your charity. And why didn't you tell me you weren't actually working at the hospital? You lied to me."

"This isn't charity. It's a job you'll get paid for. You don't have skills, so now you are in a position to obtain them. There are courses available there that can teach you what you need. Once you have those skills, by all means, move on if you feel so hard done by. Right now it's the best you'll do, outside of waitressing or bartending, and those hours are rather counterproductive for child rearing. As for my work, so what? I enjoy my job. I'm good at it. I'm in a position to help others, so I do. There is nothing wrong with that. You have a chip on your shoulder or too much pride. Either way it's a poor attitude to take."

"Oh, so I should be on my knees thanking you for the job?" I said. "Well, I would have gotten one on my own. I just needed more time."

"Pride is a terrible thing, and it won't put food on the table. Be angry if you must, but now you have a means to provide for Zoe, and an opportunity to gain some skills. That isn't wrong, and I won't apologize for it."

I turned from my post and dropped my hairnet and rubber gloves in the garbage can. I pulled on my coat, grabbed my purse, and walked out the door. The cold air turned my breath into white puffs. He was right; I wasn't getting anything but offers for waitressing. This was an opportunity, and I was being stubborn and foolish, but I couldn't help it. I reached up to pull my hair out from inside my coat collar, letting it cascade about my shoulders.

"A blond waterfall," I heard him say quietly behind me. I turned, and he gathered a fistful of hair to his face and let it drop. Then, with his hands on either side of my face, his thumbs caressed my cheekbones. I looked into his eyes, and the world stopped turning. I forgot why I was angry.

"Have you no idea how beautiful you are? Blue eyes, blond hair, delicate bone structure, slim," his voice was husky as he bent his head, his lips caressing mine slowly and gently, waiting for permission. I wound my arms around his neck, pulling him closer and the pressure of his kiss increased. When he finally pulled back, I stared into his face. My nerve endings tingled.

"Take a chance on us, Sheila," he whispered in my ear.

"Um. I...better go. Zoe, you know."

He nodded. "Don't be angry. I only wanted to help. I'll see you Tuesday."

"I start work Monday. Instead of coming here I'm going to spend my lunch with Zoe. This is my last day."

"Right. I hadn't thought of that. Good luck. You'll do well." He hesitated as if he wanted to say more, but he walked away looking back over his shoulder twice before he turned the corner.

A two-bedroom apartment opened up over the mission, and Zoe and I moved in two weeks after I started my job. Sheldon stopped by with wine and a houseplant. We shopped for second-hand furniture, went for walks in the park, made snow angels with Zoe, and when she slept we watched a movie and cuddled on the couch. Life seemed perfect.

I was at work one day when the door opened and I heard someone say, "Who is this?"

I looked up from my computer and into the icy green eyes of a statuesque brunette. She slipped out of her faux fur and flung it carelessly over the desk revealing a shapely figure in a suit buttoned in just the right places.

"Excuse me?" I asked, looking about in a vain attempt to locate the person she was speaking about then I realized it was I.

"Who — are — you." This time it wasn't a question and the words were enunciated precisely.

My mind conjured up all sorts of replies and retorts. Instead, all I said was, "My name is Sheila. I'm the new receptionist."

She stared at me pointedly, rejecting my offered hand. "Another one of Sheldon's charity cases, I see. If you're a receptionist, you'd think you could find something better to wear."

Heat rose in my cheeks. Who was this woman?

Sheldon walked through the door and she immediately strung her arm through his. "Darling, you're late," she said.

"Traffic," he replied and looked at me. "Hi Sheila, how are you? Is the job going well?"

"Oh darling, she's just the receptionist. Come, we're late for our meeting." She, whoever she was, steered Sheldon down the hall. He bent his head toward her as he was ushered out. I felt a knot in my stomach.

"Don't let Jezebel get to you," said Rachel, one of the staff counsellors. She tossed the faux fur into a chair behind the desk. "Her real name is Claire McCoy. She's wealthy and sits on various boards to prove she's important. Her main job in life is to make Sheldon's life miserable because she wants to marry him and he, so far, has been rather aloof when it comes to women. Frustrates her to no end."

"Well, Sheldon seemed pretty interested in what she had to say," I said.

A few minutes later, I took a phone message for Sheldon. It was important so I went down the hall to interrupt the meeting. Claire stood outside the door talking on her cell. She eyed me as I approached and hung up just as I got there. "Can I help you?" Her voice was cold.

"I have a message for Sheldon."

"Mr. Lamb, you mean. Really he needs to put a stop to all this. He is your boss and as such you need to treat him with more respect. I realize you are probably just off the street, but I assumed you'd know how to address your boss properly." She snatched the note from my hand.

After the meeting was over, Sheldon appeared at my desk. "Dinner tonight?" He winked. "I'll pick you and Zoe up here after work." He turned and walked off.

"So, are we seeing the great and awesome Mr. Lamb?" Rachel asked.

"Yes, we've been seeing each other, but it isn't exclusive and I rarely see him during the week now. He wants to finish up work before Christmas, but we see each other on weekends."

Two days later, I walked down the hall to the staff room. As I passed the boardroom I was surprised to see Claire sitting at the table with a file in front of her. "I didn't hear you come in, Miss McCoy. Can I get you anything? Coffee? Tea?"

"Have a seat, Mrs. Oxford," she said disdainfully. "I would like a word with you." She tapped the file with her manicured fingernail. "It seems you have difficulty keeping a husband." She raised her hand as I opened my mouth to speak. "There is nothing you need to say. I have it all here in black and white. In fact, I even saw Ted at a hospital tea last week, and he told me all about it. If you couldn't keep your husband happy, how do you ever expect to keep Sheldon happy? Was Sheldon aware you are living here in one of our homeless units? Is that why he got you a job? Was he ashamed to be seen with someone who has nothing? Not even job skills? Although it seems you're taking advantage of some of the classes offered here..." Claire rose from her seat and came to lean against the table where I sat. "You and Sheldon have not been spending time together because he and I have been together...dining, visiting friends and making plans for our engagement and wedding."

I sat in silence, holding back tears. It was true, I hadn't seen as much of Sheldon lately, but he had explained that he was working overtime to clear his calendar for the New Year. Was this the real reason I hadn't seen him?

"Let me explain how things are. Sheldon and I will be announcing our engagement at the Christmas Fundraising Dance. Then we are going on a cruise. Any romantic ideas you've had are now dust. You are nothing, and you and Sheldon are nothing." I felt her grip my arm. "Do I make myself perfectly clear?" She held out her hand to show off a beautiful diamond. "You are a guttersnipe, and Sheldon is far above you."

I shook off her hand and fled. I wanted to curl up and die. Love was blissful — and excruciatingly painful. What kind of fool was I? Back at my desk, I moved papers from one pile to another in an attempt to keep my mind busy. I felt tears well up and spill over. This was a complete disaster.

"What did Jezebel want this time? I just saw her leave by the back door. I wish she would go away and stay away..." Rachel saw my tears and immediately whisked me out of the room. "I don't know what happened but calm yourself. Maybe you need to go home for the rest of the day. Don't worry. We can cover the phones. She's got it in for you, I'm afraid, but don't let her get to you. She's rich and lonely — never a good combo." Rachel handed me a tissue and a glass of water. "I'll make arrangements for covering the front desk. Go home. We'll see you on Monday." Then she was gone.

After Zoe went to bed that night, I had never felt so alone as I stood at the window with my arms wrapped around my waist, watching the falling snow silence the world. I wanted to be furious with Sheldon, but I couldn't. I was a woman in love with a man who was in love with someone else. Being such a stand-up guy, he probably didn't know how to let me down gently. Oh, to be given the chance to begin this relationship again. I leaned against the windowpane and cried for the mistakes of the past and the pain of the present. I had no idea whom to turn to. My family was too far away, and they would only worry. I was too embarrassed to contact any of my old friends, and I hadn't made any new ones. I felt absolutely desolate.

Claire's visit explained so much. Sheldon and I were really lifestyles apart. I had lived the high life with Ted, but my reality now was at the poverty level, and I suddenly understood that the gap between Sheldon and me was insurmountable. He was probably grateful to Claire for sorting out this whole mess for him.

The next day, the phone rang, buzzed, and dinged as Sheldon left texts and phone messages. There was a knock at the door. The next day there was another series of rings, buzzes, and texts and the knocking was almost a pound. I hid behind my locked door like the coward I was and cried.

Monday morning, Rachel, standing in my spot, greeted me. "You're wanted in the board room," she said.

"I hate the board room. Nothing good ever happens for me there. Do I have to? What's it about?"

She shrugged, so I took off my coat and put down my purse. "Don't you wish you could do your job instead of mine for a change?" I asked. She smiled at me and waved me on as the phone rang.

I entered the boardroom and the door closed behind me. I whirled around to see Sheldon standing in front of the door, arms crossed at this chest.

"Have a seat. It's time for some answers."

"No thanks. Let me out, please."

"No. Sit. You and I need to talk. I don't know what's gotten into you, but you need to answer a few questions.

"I will not sit, and I will not answer your questions. If anything, you should be answering mine. You're the one who has been keeping a distance. I never see or hear from you. Why did you ask me to the dance when you and Claire were seeing each other?"

"What?"

"You two deserve each other. She's nasty and mean, and you are evil. I thought we had something. I was actually falling for you. What a fool I was. We're through." I stormed out of the room, slamming the door behind me as tears slid down my cheeks unchecked.

I was part way down the hall when an iron grip grabbed me and swung me around so fast I was flung against his chest and caught up in a tight embrace I could not escape. Finally, I just stood quietly and cried into his chest.

"You are falling for me." It was a statement and required no answer.

"*Was* falling for you," I corrected him. "I wouldn't have anything to do with you now if you were the last man on earth!" I hiccupped.

"I like the fact that you *are* falling for me, and, for your information, Claire and I haven't been seeing each other. I do have some standards. Sometimes they are a bit low, I admit, but not when it comes to the women in my life. I told you I would be out of touch except for the occasional call or text. I've been working overtime to clear my calendar for two weeks in January. I was hoping you and Zoe would join me on a cruise. While on this cruise, I was hoping you would realize you loved me and that I would fit perfectly into your family. The tickets were going to be your Christmas present. Now you've gone and spoiled that."

I pulled away from him. "Claire said you two were announcing your engagement and then going on a cruise."

"You heard me. You, me, Zoe, and two weeks on a cruise ship, someplace very warm. Claire will not be on the ship. Interested?"

I looked up at him and managed a weak smile. "A little. I thought you were announcing your engagement to Claire. She showed me an engagement ring, and she said you gave it to her. I haven't seen you, so there was no reason to disbelieve her."

"Did it not occur to you to pick up the phone? You do have my number. Maybe send a text? But I guess this isn't just your fault. I should have been in touch with you more often to tell you I was thinking of you. I know what Claire is like when she gets her claws into someone. I did not expect Claire to stop by and claim that I said I loved her."

He stopped talking and rested his cheek on top of my head, obviously not at all concerned that people were passing us in the middle of the hallway and giving us strange looks.

Finally, he started talking again. "Howard Carson has proposed and Claire has accepted. Thank goodness! He'll have his hands full. They will probably announce *their* engagement at the fundraiser. Do you realize I've already had this same conversation with Howard? I had to assure him Claire was playing games; that she and I weren't seeing each other. It's been a horrible Christmas season with those two fighting, and Claire trying to make Howard jealous. I have no idea how you women manage a love life and keep the stress under control."

"Well, we aren't usually caught in the middle," I said from the comfortable cocoon of his arms.

"Now, about us. Let's take Zoe someplace warm and spend two weeks getting to know each other. Then I say we return and see what the future holds. Are you in?"

"Yes," I answered. I pulled him closer and kissed him.

I was finally ready to take a chance on us.

SNOWED IN

Wendy Dewar Hughes

CHAPTER ONE

Pulling back the curtain, Cari studied the western sky. The weather forecast warned of heavy snow and high winds, also known as "blizzard conditions." Even if she hadn't heard the report on the noon news, she could have predicted a storm was on its way. The cattle had been milling around, turning their backs to the wind or crowding into the sheds since morning.

She dropped the curtain and grabbed her parka. Cramming her pant legs into the tops of her boots, she shoved her long blonde hair into a woolly toque and pulled it down over her ears then wrapped a scarf around her neck, stuffing the ends into the front of her jacket. If she hurried, she could get more straw down into the sheds for warmth and throw some more hay in the feed bunks before the snow started to fly.

Pulling on a pair of work gloves, Cari ran outside and hopped in the pick-up truck. Minutes later she had backed it up against the bale stack. She hopped out and scrambled to the top of the stack. Heaving straw bales into the truck's box, she leapt down after the last one and shoved them around so none would topple out before she could get into the barnyard.

After breaking the rectangular bales open and scattering the straw around with her booted feet she jumped back into the pick-up and headed out to the haystack. Tiny, hard snowflakes had already begun to swirl around her as she threw the bales into the truck and delivered them to the feed bunks.

When Cari's brother Brandon had called her the month before to ask if she could come and look after the farm while he and his wife, Sylvia, went to Mexico for Christmas she had at first turned him down. Why would she want to go back to the farm and feed cattle at Christmas when she could stay in town in her cozy apartment with her cat curled up on her lap? She could have held out, too, if he hadn't pleaded with her. Well, that and the money he offered to pay her for staying in his rambling ranch house for three weeks and looking after thirty head of cattle. Other than feeding them twice a day and making sure the heaters in the stock waterers didn't quit, causing their drinking water source to freeze, she had the remainder of the time to read books, watch television and work on her Internet business, The Travel Coach. So her cat went to stay at her neighbour's apartment and Cari drove the ninety kilometres to Brandon's ranch — the ranch where the two of them had grown up.

With the cattle fed and bedded for the night and the gate fastened, Cari parked the truck in the shop next to the workbench and plugged in the block heater. She had no intention of going anywhere tonight even though it was Christmas Eve but it didn't pay not to take all precautions against a winter storm. Fighting her way back to the house against the rising wind with needles of snow lashing her cheeks, Cari thought about spending her first Christmas ever all alone. The Barringtons down the road had invited her for Christmas dinner but she had declined. She had a low tolerance for screaming kids and smoking adults who drank too much. She preferred to have a quiet day to herself. Her little Christmas turkey already sat in cold water in the sink, thawing so she could stuff it in the morning.

Shaking the snow from her jacket and hat, she hung them on pegs behind the door and sat down on the steps that went up to the kitchen to pull her boots off. Banging the boots together, she knocked the snow off them then grabbed a broom and swept it out the door, slamming it against the cold blast that fought its way through the crack.

"Time for a fire," Cari said to no one as she poked her toes into a pair of fleece-lined slippers. Her favourite travel show was about to come on satellite television and if she hurried, she could be ensconced in the big recliner soaking up the heat from the fireplace by the time the program started. By now the wind had risen so that it moaned around the corners of the house and flung ice pellets at the windows. The skeletal branches of the poplar tree scraped against the siding like someone trying to scratch his way through the wall. Still too early for supper, the light outside had darkened so she could barely see the road running past the expanse of snow that lay outside the living room window. Cari got the fire going, turned on the television, and curled up in the armchair. If she didn't think about it too much, she hardly felt lonely at all.

Three television shows later, Cari pushed the lever on the recliner, threw a couple of more logs on the fire and went to the kitchen to scrounge for something to eat. It was hard to get excited about making meals when she was by herself in someone else's kitchen but she found a can of Mulligatawny soup in the pantry cupboard and some baking powder biscuits in the freezer. Placing the biscuits on a pan, she turned on the oven to warm them up as the soup came to a simmer on the stove.

By now darkness had fallen. Shuffling in her slippers to the dark mudroom, she cupped her hands around her eyes and peered out the window. In the glow from the yard light she could see thick snow strafing past horizontally, chased by a screaming wind. Back in the kitchen, she stirred the soup then went back the living room and picked up the TV remote. Flicking the channels, she stopped at the weather report and bit her lip as she scrutinized the maps. The reports indicated that this Arctic front had blown in from the Northwest bringing moisture from the Pacific, which turned into heavy snow because of the low temperatures. Travel warnings were in effect everywhere and viewers had been advised to stock up and hunker down for the duration.

Cari sighed. It looked like it would be a lonely Christmas indeed.

After eating her spicy soup and a few too many warm biscuits melting with butter, Cari grabbed a Christmas orange from the fridge and headed back to the fireside to watch a sitcom. She banked up the fire with lots of wood so that she wouldn't have to crawl out of that comfortable chair any time soon, and pulled a woollen throw robe over her lap.

Sometime later, Cari woke with a start. She had fallen asleep in her cozy nest as the television droned on. *What time is it?* she thought, sitting up. The room had cooled off and the fire glowed with only a few ash-covered embers. Then she heard the sound that had surely wakened her.

CHAPTER TWO

Bang, bang, thump, thump. Someone was pounding on the door and stomping on the planks of the front step. Throwing off the lap blanket, Cari scrambled out of the chair, losing a slipper on her way over the recliner's arm. She jammed her foot back in it and stumbled across the room to the kitchen. Flicking on the light in the mudroom, she pushed the flimsy curtain over the door's window out of the way and squinted into the gloom. A man stood on the step, his back to the wind and his shoulders hunched up around his ears. He wore a ball cap that Cari knew would keep his ears from freezing for approximately seven seconds in this kind of weather. *What was he thinking?* Cari twisted the door handle and yanked open the door.

"Good grief," she cried above the screech of the wind. "What are you doing out on a night like this?" She reached out and grabbed the man's parka sleeve and hauled on it. He staggered through the open door as Cari slammed it behind him.

For a moment, he just stood there stiffly, shoulders up, nostrils frosted. His clothes wore a thick layer of snow and his lower pant legs stood frozen around his boot tops. Except for the hat, he had dressed pretty well for winter weather. His entire body shuddered and he seemed to come to life.

"So, what are you doing out on a night like this?" Cari repeated as she stepped backwards up two steps so she could look straight at him. "Who are you?"

"Jack MacKenzie," he answered, pulling off a frozen glove and offering his hand to shake. Cari took it in hers and gave it a squeeze.

"Cari Graham. You're freezing," she said, rubbing his hand between both of hers now. "Give me your other one and I'll warm it up, too." He complied and after a brisk rub of both of his hands, he flexed his fingers and brushed snow from his shoulders.

"Do you mind if I come in?" he asked.

Cari stared at him. "Are you nuts? You can't go back out there. You'll die in five minutes. The temperature has dropped five degrees every hour since sundown, last time I looked. You have to come in."

"Thanks," he said, visibly relieved.

"Hold on a minute," Cari said and opened a closet near the door. She pulled out an orange heavy-duty extension cord and handed it to him. "You'd better plug in your truck or it won't start until March. There's an outlet right beside the door out there. Put this hat on first, though." She handed him the woolly toque she'd worn earlier.

A minute later he was back, looking almost as frozen as before.

"Take off your coat and hang it there," Cari instructed. "It can drip on the rug. I'll grab you some slippers to put on. I'm sure your feet could use warming up, too."

She ran off to the bedroom that Brandon and Sylvia shared and rummaged around in the closet until she unearthed a pair of grubby knitted slippers. *Brandon wears these things?* she thought, then shrugged and headed back to the stranger. "These are the best I could do," she explained, handing the slippers to Jack. "They're stretchy so you should be able to get your feet in them." The visitor stood a good head taller than her younger brother so chances were his feet were bigger than Brandon's.

"Perfect," Jack said after he stuffed his feet into the slippers. He grinned at Cari, his cheeks bright red from cold and windburn.

"Well, you'd better come in since you're not going anywhere else tonight. Perhaps now you can answer my question."

"I work for an oil well service," Jack explained, following Cari into the kitchen. "I was out checking a well when the weather turned and by the time I started heading back towards town the visibility was so bad I couldn't see past my front bumper. I saw the yard light through the snow and thought I'd better pull in. The last thing a guy wants is to be stranded in a ditch in a blizzard. It would be days before anyone found me."

Cari shivered. "There's a gruesome thought," she said. "Have you eaten? I've got some left-over soup I can re-heat and a half dozen biscuits that will only take a few minutes to warm."

Jack seemed to brighten at the mention of food, as though suddenly reminded of just how long he'd been hungry. "That would be great," he said. "I haven't eaten for hours. Do you mind if I sit down?"

"Be my guest," Cari replied, gesturing toward a chair at the kitchen table. She turned on the burner under the pot of leftover soup and placed the biscuits back in the oven on low heat. "I hope you didn't have elaborate plans for Christmas," she said, making conversation. "It doesn't look like you'll be going anywhere for a while."

Jack ran his hands through a mop of brown hair pushing it away from his forehead. Squinting up at Cari, he said, "No, I'm scheduled to work over the holidays. Most of the other guys have families so they wrangled the best days off. My folks are too far away for me to go home for a few days and I have no other family around here. What about you? Are you here by yourself or is there a husband somewhere?" He glanced over his shoulder as though someone might materialize out of one of the appliances.

Cari laughed. "I'm holding down the fort here for my brother and his wife who flew off to Mexico for the holidays. I've got cattle down in the pens to feed and water every day. I was expecting a pretty quiet Christmas. I've got my little turkey thawing for tomorrow though." She gave the bird a poke, sending it bobbing around in the water-filled sink, "so we'll be able to have a nice dinner."

When the soup began to bubble, Cari ladled it into a soup bowl and set it on the table in front of Jack. By now his cheek colour had gone from bright red to pink. Taking the biscuits from the oven, she placed a pile of them on a plate and set the butter dish next to it. "This ought to help," she said, sitting across the table from him.

For a while, Jack ate in silence, wolfing down biscuits as though he might not get another meal. Cari felt sure he must have burned his mouth on the soup but she didn't mention it. She glanced up at the clock, surprised to see that it read 9:35 already. How long had she slept?

"Oh, man, was that ever good!" Jack said as he mopped the remaining drops of soup from his bowl with a piece of biscuit. "I didn't realize how hungry I was."

"Do you have any stuff in your truck you need to bring in?" Cari asked, taking Jack's dishes and placing them in the dishwasher. She didn't need to ask what kind of vehicle he drove. Everyone in the country drove pick-up trucks, especially oilfield workers. Oil pumping stations littered the surrounding prairie, which sat atop massive oil and natural gas reserves. Local towns boomed with the business created by the oil patch and its multiple spin-off industries. New hotels seemed to pop up every month to accommodate transient oil workers and the families that came with them looking for homes near an abundance of jobs.

"No," Jack replied. "Nothing I need to keep from freezing. I hadn't planned to stop for the night anywhere. Everything I have is in town."

Cari offered him a Mandarin orange and some ginger cookies that she had found in the freezer the previous day that Sylvia had baked for her to eat. Jack accepted her offer of the food followed by a cup of coffee.

"Your pants are wet from being out in the weather," Cari commented when Jack stood to his feet. "Why don't you come into the living room and I'll put some more wood on the fire so you can dry off. It won't take long once the coals heat up."

Jack followed her into the living room and went over to stand by the plate glass window as she banked the fire. The little Christmas tree that Cari had put up and decorated the day before stood in the corner, its lights twinkling cheerily. She had almost decided to skip the tree this year but when she had gone into town, she had walked past a tree lot and spotted this scraggly stray standing by itself in a corner. It looked so forlorn she couldn't leave it there. "If we're going to be lonely," she had said to the tree as she carried it to the cash register, "we might as well be lonely together."

"It's a wild night out there," Jack said, staring at the whirling snow. "I'm sure glad I happened upon your place. I'm sorry to barge in on you like this though. I don't suppose you were expecting company."

Cari laughed as she drew the screen across in front of the leaping flames to keep the sparks off the wood floor. "No, I wasn't expecting company," she agreed, "but nobody out in this country turns away a traveller when the weather is bad." She stood up and rubbed her hands on her pant legs.

Jack turned away from the window to face her. "You have nothing to fear from me, you know," he said. "I really appreciate you taking me in but I want you to know you're in no danger. I won't hurt you. I'm not that kind of guy."

Cari hadn't realized that she'd been carrying tension across her shoulders since he'd arrived but now it let go and her muscles relaxed. She nodded. "I sensed that," she said, "but I appreciate you saying it. Now, if you'll help me pull that sectional over here you can stretch your legs out toward the fire and we can watch the late news if you like. Then I'll show you where you can sleep tonight. This house has lots of rooms so you can take your pick."

Together they moved the furniture to a more comfortable position and Jack stretched his legs toward the fire. No sooner had the news come on than he fell asleep. Cari watched it for a little while but lost interest and turned it off. The light from the flames flickered over Jack's features as Cari sat motionless, studying him. He looked to be around her age, early thirties. His skin, now that the redness had faded, showed that he spent plenty of time outdoors. Dark brows framed his eyes with their short dark lashes and he had a straight nose and nice lips. Her eyes lingered on his lips for a second longer than she had intended and he stirred in his sleep. She snatched her gaze away then looked back at him to find that he'd woken and lay watching her with hazel eyes. For a few moments, neither of them spoke. He then sat up and pushed his hands through his hair.

"I fell asleep," he said unnecessarily and turned his head to look at Cari. "If you don't mind directing me to a bed, I wouldn't mind hitting the hay. It's been a long day."

CHAPTER THREE

Cari woke with a start. Had she heard something? She listened intently. The winter wind still howled as it rounded the corners of the house. In the pearly grey light of dawn she could see snow still slashing sideways. She slid out of bed, pushed her toes into slippers then grabbed the afghan from the bed and wrapped it around her shoulders. Standing next to the bedroom window, she peered into the gloom. A glance at the clock told her it was morning even though between being one of the shortest days of the year and the heavy snowfall outside, it still looked dark outside.

Tiptoeing out to the hallway, she turned up the thermostat then dressed in long underwear, jeans, an undershirt, a long-sleeved t-shirt, a wool pullover and two pairs of socks. She had to check on the cattle before breakfast.

As Cari sat on the landing steps pulling on her snow boots, Jack came up the stairs from the basement.

"Merry Christmas," Cari said. "Did you sleep well?"

"Like you wouldn't believe. Where are you going?"

"Cattle," Cari answered, reaching for her parka. "They wait for no woman. I have to feed them and make sure the waterers haven't frozen overnight."

"I'll help." Jack bounded up the last couple of steps and grabbed his coat.

"You don't have to do that," Cari protested.

"Do you honestly expect me to sit in here while you're out there feeding livestock? Besides, in this kind of weather anything could happen. You might need me." He grinned up at her as he stuffed his pant legs into his boots.

She smiled back. "You need a better hat than that wimpy oil company thing you had on last night." She opened a cupboard and pulled out a fur-lined hat with long earflaps. "Here, wear this one. It will preserve your ears for your later years."

Leaning into the raging wind, Jack and Cari walked side by side to the shop where she unplugged her block heater and turned the key in the pick-up's ignition. The engine protested with a groan but then started. The two of them sat in the cab while it warmed up enough to drive.

"I hope we can get to the bale stacks with this or I'll have to get out the tractor and push some snow around first."

"You do that kind of work?" Jack asked, looking at her.

Cari raised her eyebrows. *What kind of a question is that?* "Uh, yeah," she said. "Do you see anyone else here?"

Backing the pick-up out of the shop, Cari turned it toward the hay yard. A low snowdrift had blocked the road but she stomped on the gas pedal and powered through it. Around the bale stacks and the cowsheds, snow had drifted in towering crescents, rooftop high, but the driving wind had blown the open stretches of the hay yard clear. Together, Cari and Jack fed the cattle and chopped the ice forming around the perimeters of the heated waterers.

"Thanks for helping me," Cari said when they blew back through the door of the house later. "It goes way faster with two people."

"Let me help you with that," Jack said, reaching for the scarf wound around Cari's neck. "You're covered with snow and it's all going to fall down your neck in a second."

After getting out of layers of outdoor gear, Cari said, "I've got bacon, eggs, hash browns and multi-grain toast for breakfast. I think there's even some Saskatoon berry jam here. Hungry?"

Jack grinned. "I could eat a steer."

"Sorry, those guys are not on the menu."

After breakfast Jack volunteered to clean up the kitchen and Cari slipped into the bedroom to take off her extra layers of clothing. With feeding the cattle and making breakfast, she had almost forgotten that it was Christmas morning but now she realized that while she had a few gifts under the tree tagged for her, from her parents and brother, there would be nothing for Jack. Digging into the bottom of her suitcase, she pulled out a book that she had bought for herself. Her plan was to indulge some of her travel dreams using the book of hundreds of places everyone should visit as her guide. She flipped it open and riffled the pages. She could get herself another copy. In the hall closet, Cari found Christmas wrap, ribbons and tape. In minutes, the book had been wrapped and tagged with Jack's name on it. Sneaking out toward the living room, she tiptoed past while his back was turned and placed the gift under the tree.

"How's it going?" she asked nonchalantly as she wandered back into the kitchen. "Did you remember that today is Christmas?"

Jack dried his hands on a tea towel. "I guess it is. Merry Christmas."

"I thought I'd open the gifts now, if that's all right with you. I have a few from my family."

"Sure, that sounds like fun." He hung up the towel and followed her to the living room doorway where she stood waiting for him.

"I didn't get anything for you," he said. "I wasn't exactly planning to be here." He shifted awkwardly from one foot to the other then glanced up. A wilted sprig of mistletoe hung from a ribbon above Cari's head.

She followed his gaze. Then her eyes met his.

"About all I have to offer is a Christmas kiss," he said. Before she could comment, he lowered his lips to hers and placed one soft kiss there. "It's not much," he said afterwards, "but I hardly know you." With a twinkle in his eyes he added, "But if this blizzard keeps up, who knows…"

With the sensation of his lips on hers lingering, Cari slid her arm through his and said, "Come on, let's tear some paper."

She opened her gifts first—a camera tripod from her brother and Sylvia, and a hand-knit pure alpaca wool sweater from her parents.

"Oh, look," Cari exclaimed. "Here's one for you. It has your name on it." She handed Jack the gift that she had wrapped only minutes before.

Hi brow furrowed. "How can that be?" he said. "No one knows I'm even here." He took it from Cari.

"Open it," she said.

Jack tore the paper off and gazed at the book. "That's incredible! I've been thinking of buying this book for a long time. How did…? It's from you, isn't it?"

"Yes, it's from me," she said, smiling at him. "I couldn't bear the thought of you being here without a gift on Christmas morning."

CHAPTER FOUR

After opening gifts, Cari prepared the stuffing for the turkey while Jack thumbed through his new book at the kitchen table. She filled the turkey's cavity and put the bird into the oven then set a canning jar of her mother's Christmas Carrot Pudding into a pan of simmering water.

"Have you ever been to Sri Lanka?" Jack asked, studying a page in the book.

"Nope. Have you?"

"No, but someday I want to go there."

Cari tilted her head and looked at him. "Me too." She pulled a chair around beside him and sat down, looking over his arm at the photos.

"Here," he said, sliding the open book her way. "We can look at it together. By the way, I've told you what I do for a job. What do you do?"

Cari explained that in her business as a travel coach, she helped her clients navigate through the possible complications of foreign and adventure travel, as well as writing a blog and publishing guidebooks and short videos for travellers.

"You've probably been nearly everywhere then," Jack said, searching her face.

"Not everywhere yet but lots of places. I have to check things out so I can help other people. After Christmas I'm going to Fiji and Samoa."

Jack looked at her with admiration. "You're kind of intrepid, aren't you? No wonder you're not fazed by feeding cattle in a blizzard." He went back to flipping pages.

After a feast of turkey, stuffing, roasted garlic mashed potatoes, gravy, Brussels sprouts with pecans, and glazed carrots, they topped off Christmas dinner with Cari's mom's pudding with lemon sauce.

When the clean-up was done, Jack ambled into the living room and rolled into the recliner. "That was the best Christmas dinner I think I've ever had," he said, rubbing a hand over his rounded belly. "You sure can cook!"

Cari settled on the sofa and put her feet up. "I'm a farm girl," she said. "We have to learn to do just about everything." They subsided into overstuffed silence and within minutes both fell asleep.

Cari woke a while later and nudged Jack's foot. "It's time to feed the steers again," she announced when he opened his eyes.

Jack didn't hesitate. "On it," he said, blinking and pushing himself to his feet.

Outside, the snowfall seemed to have stepped up and the wind still ripped at their faces. When she pulled the truck up to the cattle pen gate, she discovered that it was open.

"Oh no," she cried. "The wind must have loosened the latch." Once in the cattle pen, Cari counted animals. "I'm missing eight head," she shouted, shielding her face from the wind as she counted again. "They must have gotten out. We have to find them."

Jack wrapped his arms around her. Placing his mouth close to her ear he said, "We can't go looking for them. The drifts are too high for the truck and we'd die of cold in minutes if we got lost walking around. They'll be all right. Come on back to the house."

"No, Jack," Cari wailed. "Brandon will be devastated if I lose his cattle."

Jack's strong arm guided Cari back toward the truck. "He'll be a lot more devastated if he loses his sister in a blizzard. Come on now. We have to go in. The cows will find their own shelter."

By the time they had made it back to the shop, darkness loomed. The wind seemed to grow even stronger at dusk and the two of them clung to each other as they fought their way against the gusts to the house.

"It even seems colder in here," Cari said, once she had shed her winter gear. "I'm going to get the fire going and make us some hot apple cider."

"I'll do the fire," Jack offered. "You make the cider."

She could hear him tossing logs onto the grate and then caught the crackle of kindling. "Here you go," Cari said, walking into the living room and handing Jack a steaming mug of cider, complete with a cinnamon stick. The fire now blazed and the heat felt good on her cold limbs. Snuggling into the sofa, she pulled the woolly throw up over her legs and wrapped her hands around her own mug. Jack sat down next to her.

"Do you mind if we snuggle? My legs feel like ice." Cari flipped the blanket over his form and he pulled her close under his arm. "That's better," he said. "I think this is one of the nicest Christmases I've ever had. How about you?"

She tilted her head so she could look at his face. *Was it?* Thoughts swirled through her mind. She really liked this guy. *He's smart; he's cute; he's thoughtful.* And she couldn't deny the attraction she felt for him. Sitting here, all cozy by the fire, she had to admit, it all felt pretty great. "I don't think it gets much better than this," she said.

A moment later, he kissed her—a long, slow, sweet kiss. And a moment after that, the house went completely dark. The power had gone out.

CHAPTER FIVE

"Oh, no," Cari cried, throwing off the blanket and starting to get up. Jack pulled her back down.

"Just sit tight for a minute," he suggested. "It might come back on."

The fire blazed just past their feet as they sat and waited. Minutes ticked by. Jack pulled Cari closer.

"The furnace won't work when the power's off," she said.

"I know," he replied.

"Neither will the cattle waterers."

"I know. They can eat snow."

She looked at him.

"In any case, they'll make it until morning. This storm has to blow itself out soon and we can carry water or break ice in the morning, right?"

"I guess so."

"In that case," Jack said, "the only thing we need to do is stay warm. I can keep the fire going all night."

Cari leaned her head against his shoulder. "I'm assuming you mean the one in the fireplace," she said.

He drew back far enough to look in her eyes. "I'm probably one of the last honourable men alive," he said earnestly. "I want to get to know you, not take advantage of this situation. Well," he corrected himself, "part of me wants to take advantage of it but the intelligent part won't let me."

She smiled and kissed his cheek. "Me too," she replied. "Tell me your story."

Cari awoke the next morning to the sound of a heavy-duty motor vehicle. She opened her eyes to see sunlight blazing through the living room windows. The air in the house felt still and polar but the minute she sat up on the sofa, the lights and the furnace all came on. Jack stirred beside her, yawned, and rubbed his eyes. Looking around, he seemed to be trying to remember where he was then threw the blanket off and stood up.

"Good morning," Cari said. "The blizzard has stopped."

"I'd better put more wood on the fire," Jack said.

"No need. The power came back on a minute ago."

"Okay then. What's that sound?" Jack sprang to the window and looked out. "It's the plough! They're clearing the roads." His shoulders sagged. "That means I'll have to go back to work."

"And it was so much more fun feeding cattle in a blizzard here with me," Cari joked. "I know—that's hard to top."

Jack turned back to Cari; then in what seemed like one move, leapt over the back of the sofa and landed beside her. He wrapped his arms around her and kissed her soundly. "It's impossible to top!"

"Well," Cari said. "There's only one thing to do. We'll have to keep a close eye on the forecast for the next couple of weeks. As soon as they start talking about 'snow and blowing snow,' you get yourself out here."

Jack laughed. "I have a better idea. Why don't we have dinner together in town tomorrow? I'm sure you'll be tired of turkey leftovers by then and I'll have an official day off."

"I'd like that," Cari said. "Now, if you'll get moving, I have cattle to find and feed."

AUTHORS

Barbara Glover is a published author who lives and works in Brandon, Manitoba Canada. Barb grew up a farm girl involved in 4-H, and farm life, however, she much preferred a warm corner and a book. Once high school was completed she went to university where she obtained her Bachelor of Social Work. After university, Barb moved to northern Manitoba to work in Churchill and Thompson then moved back to Brandon so her daughter could attend school. After returning to Brandon, Barb worked to obtain her MSW.

Barb has taken online courses through Winghill Writing School, Manitoba Writer's Guild, and York University. Barb has taken The Art of Managing Your Career with Heather Bishop, and is currently mentoring with Suzanne Lieurance, and is a member of the Manitoba Writer's Guild, CANSCAIP, and ACI Manitoba.

Barb's hobbies include quilting, knitting, painting, and she is an avid reader and writer. It isn't unusual to find Barb's social work experience seeping into the short stories she writes. Barb has a passion for weight lifting. She has taken many interesting canoe and camping trips with her husband Warren. Always wanting to learn something new Barb is researching fairy gardens in the hopes of growing one in her back yard.

This is Barb's first attempt at writing romance.

Barb can be reached at barbglover4@yahoo.ca and look for her on Facebook.

Suzanne Lieurance is an award-winning author, freelance writer, writing coach, speaker and workshop presenter. She is a former classroom teacher and was an instructor for the Institute of Children's Literature for over eight years.

Lieurance has written over two dozen published books, including *Write a Romance in 5 Simple Steps*, and her articles and stories have appeared in various magazines, newsletters, and newspapers, such as *Family Fun, Instructor, New Moon for Girls, KC Weddings, The Journal of Reading*, and *Children's Writer* to name a few.

Lieurance offers a variety of coaching programs via private phone calls, teleclasses, listserv, and private email for writers who want to turn their love of writing (for children and/or adults) into a part-time or full-time career. She is also president and founder of The Working Writer's Club at www.workingwritersclub.com (membership in the club is free).

Suzanne Lieurance offers *The Morning Nudge*, every weekday morning to writers via email. Get your free subscription at www.morningnudge.com.

Suzanne Lieurance divides her time between Tennessee and the beaches of Florida.

Wendy Dewar Hughes writes award-winning, inspirational suspense novels set in contemporary times. Her fiction inspires and entertains readers with compelling plots, fascinating characters and satisfying romance. The Jill Moss Adventures series includes the titles, *Picking up the Pieces*, and *The Glass Dolphin*. She is currently working on the third book in the series entitled, *Indigo Beach*. Visit http://www.jillmossadventures.com.

Wendy Dewar Hughes also writes non-fiction on spiritual topics as in her book, *Turning on the Light – Finding Your Sweet Place in the Spirit*.

As well as being an author, Wendy Dewar Hughes is a book mentor and writing coach. Her company, Summer Bay Press, offers writing programs designed to help writers complete book projects quickly. She is also a professional artist and graphic designer who creates custom-designed book covers, interior book design and e-book formatting. For more information on writing and publishing your book, see http://www.summerbaypress.com.

Wendy is also the founder of Passport to Brilliance where she publishes Creative Inspirations Daily email. For a free subscription, visit http://www.passporttobrilliance.com.

Wendy Dewar Hughes also licenses her artwork, which appears on products that are sold throughout the world. Wendy's website is http://www.wendydewarhughes.com.

Wendy Dewar Hughes lives in British Columbia, Canada.